the SOUL thief

THE GYPSY DREAMWALKER. BOOK ONE

the SOUL thief

THE GYPSY DREAMWALKER. BOOK ONE

DAVID MENEFEE

Sophic Arts
2014

Printed in the United States of America
First Printing: 2014

ISBN: 069221772X
ISBN-13: 978-0692217726

Sophic Arts
PO Box 1183
Hayfork, CA 96041
www.SophicArts.com

DEDICATION

This book is dedicated to Aset,
Beloved Teacher
Healer
Friend

ACKNOWLEDGMENTS

First, this book would never have been written without the gracious and loving support of my partner Rachel. Thank you, love. My writing group gave me a much-needed kick start to propel this work out of its dusty drawer and onto my desk. Thank you, Andrea, Zachary and Rachel! Finally, I would never have considered publishing this book without the ever-patient work by my editor, Sarah Carleton, and my proofreader, Jenn Zaczek, both of Red Adept Publishing. A deep bow of gratitude to you.

CAT

GREEN-eyed cat
With claws of jagged glass
Tear my eyes
And take my hateful sight
Let me pass
To thankful rest tonight.
Green-eyed cat
With fangs of wicked steel
Rip my ears
And silence my mind fill.
Set me free
For voices cage my will.
Green-eyed cat
With fur of ashen gray
Stop my mouth
And end my pain-filled life
No more day.
No more hate and bitter endless strife
- C

PROLOGUE

THE MAN in the Armani suit tipped the taxi driver very well before getting out of the cab, in obedience to the voice in his head. As the vehicle pulled away, the man stood on the sun-drenched sidewalk and looked up at the Gothic edifice of the hospital, his hands deep in his pockets. After a moment, he shambled toward the open front gate in the high, wrought-iron fence that surrounded the hospital, stumbling once on the slightly uneven pavement. He stopped before entering the grounds and stared at the arch over the gate, on which were spelled out the words of the Latin motto: *Aversos compono animos.*

The voice spoke to him. —*Go in*—

After a moment, he lowered his gaze to the sidewalk and entered the hospital grounds. He shuffled to where the sidewalk intersected a walkway that circled the hospital building. Turning left, he proceeded toward the west wing. An orderly was pushing a wheelchair-bound patient on the walkway in his direction, but he ignored them and maintained his slow pace.

The orderly had stopped. "Excuse me, sir."

The man collided with the wheelchair and staggered. The orderly swore and backed up. The man glanced at the orderly and then stepped aside.

"Watch where you're going next time!" The orderly swore again, shaking his head, and resumed his round.

—*A little farther. She cannot have you, and you cannot have her... but I shall let her see you anyway.*—

The man walked steadily until he reached a bench positioned directly across from a barred window.

—*Sit.*—

He sat, facing the hospital.

—*Now, give yourself to me. I have taken your artist's talent already. There is nothing left for you.*—

The man dug into his right pants pocket and pulled out a bottle of pills. He stared at the label with its dosage information and his name printed on it. Roger Charles. His name was Roger Charles. He twisted off the childproof cap and shook two capsules into his palm. He closed his hand over them, squeezing until his fist shook, then opened it to let the pills fall to the ground. He emptied the rest of the bottle and dropped it, staring directly at the window across the lawn from where he sat.

"Angela..." He reached into his jacket pocket, withdrew a snub-nosed .38 revolver, lifted the gun to his temple, and pulled the trigger.

1.

TWENTY-SEVEN *Hours Earlier*

"Oh God. It's coming! Help me! It's eating me!" The teenaged girl screamed and twisted convulsively on the gurney. She sagged and stared at Dr. Lindquist. "Get me out of here," she whispered hoarsely. A nurse used the lull in the struggle to administer a sedative, and the girl's eyes fluttered as it took effect.

As an orderly finished strapping her down, Dr. Josef Lindquist stood over her gurney, absentmindedly tugging his neatly trimmed goatee with one hand. She was very thin, with sweat-dampened black hair and an olive complexion. Dressed in a hospital gown that was tangled with her legs, she looked very frail, belying the vigor with which she had resisted the orderlies.

"Tell me about this one," said Lindquist. "What am I looking at?"

"She's one of the transfers from Lindon," replied the nurse. She checked her clipboard. "Cassandra Grey. Eighteen years old. Seems she's a poet." She showed Lindquist a much-scribbled-on bundle of dirty, partly damp paper and cardboard.

He ignored it but took the clipboard she offered him. He flipped a page. "They have diagnosed her as delusional with dissociative tendencies." He smiled primly. "She will do nicely. Put her in Seclusion Room Three and keep her sedated. I'll be back after my meeting, in half an hour."

He scribbled on the admissions form on the clipboard, handed it back to the nurse, and stalked out the door. Once outside of the emergency room, he made his way through the busy main ward, dodging the hospital's frantic activity. The noise made him wince. The morning had been unusually busy since overflow patients had arrived on a secure shuttle from Lindon Mental Health Center in Los Angeles.

Lindquist continued along a tall-ceilinged corridor toward the administrative wing. He paid little attention to the gothic architecture and archaic plaster walls that had fascinated him when he first took over as administrator, three years before. However, the echoing voices and clatter of gurneys made him glance up at the ceiling and wish, not for the first time, that it was made of acoustic tile instead of stone.

Franklin Psychiatric Hospital sprawled on one of San Francisco's picturesque hills, an incongruous gothic edifice towering over the more modern buildings to either side. Occupying most of a city block, it was a West Coast version of New York City's Bellevue. Barred windows accentuated its status as the first destination for the mentally ill, most of whom spent no more than a day there before being released again.

When the wind from the north blew, it whipped among the spiked crenellations and crouching gargoyles, whistled across the tiled roof, and probed the colossal pile of gothic architecture as if attempting to jostle it awake. Generations of pigeons had streaked the walls below the gutters, and a community of bats had made their home in the gaps that had opened up under the roof of one of the towers.

As a visitor approached the always-open iron gate leading to the hospital grounds, she would notice the hospital's motto, *Aversos compono animos*—"I bring relief to troubled minds"—wrought in the arch above. Within the high fence, the tidy lawn, sidewalks, and concrete benches conveyed that it was a park-like and pleasant facility, but nothing could mitigate the hospital's ominous facade. The stone cherubs set above the hospital entrance also failed to soften its appearance.

Pushing open the heavy wooden doors, this visitor would find a high-ceilinged foyer decorated with tall potted plants, whose vintage architecture brought to mind one of the turn-of-the-century grand hotels that had long since fallen on hard times. The huge admissions counter facing the entrance was typically staffed with clerks and nurses, while brawny orderlies were conspicuously available in case the visitor should prove violent.

To the right of the admissions counter, two wooden doors marked "Staff Only" led to the administrative offices. In the unlikely event that the visitor would be allowed to walk unaccompanied through those doors, she would find the area quiet, except for the sound of footsteps echoing on the tile floors. The high ceilings and cool, dim light would remind her of a government establishment.

To the left of the admissions counter was a third door made of steel that led into the rest of the hospital. The halls beyond that door were not so quiet. Upon opening the door, the visitor would immediately hear sounds of human distress. Distant shouts, moans, and other unidentifiable noises could travel throughout the hospital, due to its stone construction and ultra-reflective acoustics. Yet, although it might sound like a madhouse, it was, in fact, a well-regulated and calm facility, thanks to the use of modern drugs and seclusion rooms. While the use of restraints and seclusion was increasingly controversial elsewhere in the modern world of psychiatric intervention, Franklin Psychiatric relied extensively on those techniques to control often-violent individuals culled from the streets of San Francisco and the greater Bay Area as well as transferees from Los Angeles.

If she were admitted as a patient, the unlucky visitor might find herself bound securely to a hospital bed by wrists and ankles (the "four-point" binding system), or she might simply be confined to a plain room with padded walls, a single mattress, and a small narrow window, usually high on the wall, with sunlight wanly streaming through the screen and between its bars. If she were a fortunate inmate who had no violent tendencies, she would be ensconced in a more comfortable bed with modern amenities and an unobstructed view of the grounds.

Were she a tourist who had miraculously bypassed the hospital police and other security measures to wander unaccompanied through this place, she would soon find herself confronting nurses and orderlies, all on the alert to guide such an unfortunate back to the public part of the building. On the way, were she sensitive, she might feel the collected emotional impressions of countless distressed people permeating the walls, and her mood would sink to such an extent that soon she would find that she might need to check in after all. However, if she resisted such an urge, she would find herself courteously escorted back into the foyer where, relieved, she could escape to the outside world of San Francisco and freedom.

2.

Warm sunlight streamed through barred windows, causing the dust in the air to fluoresce in the treatment room. Dr. Angela Cooper, Attending Psychiatrist in the Emergency Ward, pulled back a privacy curtain. Her patient was sitting at the edge of the bed. Angela picked up the clipboard from the hook at the foot of the bed. "So, Roger. Off your meds again?"

"Sorry, Angela. I can't paint very well when I take 'em." He grinned ruefully. "But after I fought with my star pupil and nearly shoved his paintbrush up his... wherever... I knew I had to check in again."

She shook her head. "That's what happens when you stop taking your pills. Look, do me a favor and stay on the meds, okay? We can cut back the dosage soon, I promise."

"Yeah, boss." Roger hopped off of the bed.

Angela handed him the clipboard. "Just sign here and take the scrip to the pharmacy."

He scribbled on the form and took the paper she handed him. He froze in place for a moment, holding the paper.

"You can't hide from me," he mumbled.

Angela looked at him, confused. "What did you say?"

Roger stared at her. "What?"

"You said something about hiding from you."

"No, I didn't."

"Never mind. Get on those meds and take care of yourself."

He raised one hand in a wry salute and left the room. She gathered the rest of the paperwork and followed him. As she closed the door, she saw Josef in the hallway walking briskly from the direction of the emergency room. Taking a deep breath and gripping her paperwork, she intercepted him. "Dr. Lindquist, we need to talk."

Josef waited for her, his face set in an expression of detached annoyance. "Make it quick. I've got a meeting in five minutes."

"All right, then," Angela said. "Any idea when I'll get those interns?"

"I have already told you; there will be a delay. We're waiting on a grant, and there are other priorities I need to deal with first."

A passing nurse handed Angela a form. She scanned it, signed it, and handed it back. She could feel her irritation with Josef growing. "I need those interns now! Is there anything you can do?"

"Talk to me again in a couple of days, Dr. Cooper. I'll have more information for you then."

"You said that last week. And the week before that."

Josef frowned, tugging his goatee. "I wish I could tell you more, but my hands are tied. I promise you I will have more information tomorrow."

Angela had heard that before, too. She knew she would not get anything more from Josef today. "Okay. I'll hold you to it."

They parted ways, and Angela continued to the admissions foyer. Pushing open the swinging doors, she saw several street-worn men seated on the stained, overstuffed chairs. The guys looked out of place amongst the potted plants and overflowing coffee tables. She approached the nurse station window.

"What've you got for me?"

The nurse checked the computer. "Let's see. I've added a bipolar and two more patients returning for follow-up." She handed Angela a sheet for her clipboard. Taking it, Angela sighed, feeling her energy drain away, then squared her shoulders.

"Okay. Looks like I'm pulling another late shift."

She reached up and tugged her thick black hair more tightly into its ponytail before leaving the nurse's station to start her rounds. Glancing at the sheet as she walked, she noticed that the first patient on her list, the new arrival, had been picked up by the police yesterday. The hospital could only keep him for three days, the maximum allowed by law without certification, and it was up to her to evaluate his condition and, if necessary, admit him for up to two more weeks. According to the record, he was code gray, a potentially violent patient, so she would need to recruit orderlies and a nurse, the latter to administer sedative if needed.

The seclusion room was upstairs, and rather than ride the groaning, antiquated elevator, Angela took the stairs. She always preferred the graceful stone banisters and marble steps to the wrought iron and rattling steel plates of the ancient Otis. On her way up, she paused for a moment at the midpoint landing to look out the window at the San Francisco skyline, one of her favorite sights. Then, taking two steps at a time to get her heart pumping, she continued to the second floor. Turning left at the landing, she proceeded along the corridor, pausing to wait for a gurney being wheeled into one of the rooms, and approached the nurse station. "Hey, Margaret," she said, greeting the duty nurse. "I've got a code gray in Seclusion Room Eight. Can you grab a couple of orderlies and a nurse for me?"

Margaret, a thin woman in her fifties, nodded then held up a hand for a moment as she punched an intercom button. "Orderlies needed at Seclusion Room Eight. Code gray." She looked up at Angela and smiled. "On their way."

"Thanks." Angela continued strolling until, reaching the seclusion room, she paused outside the door and checked the chart mounted there. Kelly, aged fifty-eight, a homeless veteran. She shook her head. If he refused oral medication, she could do nothing unless he demonstrated that he was a danger to self or others.

When the orderlies and nurse arrived five minutes later, Angela unlocked the door and let the orderlies go in first before following with the nurse.

Kelly was hunched, unmoving, on the plain cot, his face in his hands. He was dressed in a hospital gown and pants, with a light-blue identification ribbon on his right wrist.

"Kelly?" Angela's voice was light and even. "How're you doing?"

The man was silent. The burly orderlies stood to one side, in a carefully chosen, nonthreatening posture, while the nurse waited by Angela's elbow.

"Kelly, I need you to—"

Kelly's head snapped up, and he glared at Angela. "You don't have no right to keep me here."

"The police brought you. If you'll work with me, I can release you soon." She indicated the nurse. "The nurse here has an oral sedative that I need you to—"

"Shut the fuck up, bitch."

The orderlies became watchful, and Angela knew to keep her tone detached. "Kelly..."

He rose abruptly and lunged at Angela. The orderlies swiftly intercepted him, grabbed his wrists, and pinned him back down on the bed. The move seemed effortless, and Kelly offered no resistance, nor did he say another word, as they fastened restraints around his wrists and ankles. The nurse came forward then with a ready hypodermic, a large one preloaded with Inapsine. With practiced ease, she administered the shot high on his left buttock.

As the sedative took hold, Kelly locked gazes with Angela. There was a pleading in his eyes that struck through her businesslike calm.

What personal demons are you wrestling with now, Kelly? What's going on behind those eyes, behind that forehead?

Shaking herself out of her reverie, and noting that Kelly had fallen into a drowsy torpor, she scribbled on his chart and signaled the others to follow her out of the room. According to his case history, Kelly had been picked up by the police after passersby complained about his threats and shouting. He was another reject of society, and the tragedy was that he, like so many veterans, had been abandoned by the country that he had served and left to wander the streets.

"I think I'll certify him for a 5250," Angela told the nurse as she walked back to the station. This was the code for a two-week involuntary admission.

"What do you think? Think your protocol could cure him?"

They stopped at the nurse station. Angela rubbed her face, already weary at the start of this long day. "You know, I think so. You should've seen the guy I treated back east a couple of weeks ago. Full-blown schizophrenia, and after just a week he was nearly asymptomatic. No drugs at all."

The nurse whistled. "Damn."

Angela gave her the paperwork, and the nurse began keying the latest patient notes into the hospital's antiquated database. Angela rested her elbows on the high desk. "I envy the hospital that gets to run the clinical trial."

The nurse looked up from the keyboard. "Why can't we run it? You designed it."

Angela shook her head. "We're understaffed here. Radiatrics wants a well-equipped facility to test their rTMS. I tried to talk 'em into it, but they were pretty adamant."

The nurse finished her data entry. "Here you go."

"Thanks. Maybe if the trials are held here in California, I can transfer Kelly. It sucks, what happened to him and the other vets."

She left the nurse to continue her rounds. There were twelve patients to see, both returnees and new arrivals. By the end of the day, she was mentally and emotionally exhausted. It was Monday, and ordinarily Angela would go home after work to spend some quality time with a book, but despite her fatigue, she was feeling restless. After gathering up her backpack in her office, she visited the emergency ward's nursing station. "Hey, Ginny." Nurse Virginia Delaney, a cheerful, round-faced woman, looked up from her desk.

"Hi, Angela. Just a sec; I've got to answer this." Ginny picked up the phone with one hand while she finished gathering up her belongings with the other. "No, don't move anyone tonight. We can talk about it tomorrow. My shift's ending and I've got to get home." She hung up and looked at Angela, giving her a forced smile.

"Ah, never mind," Angela said. "I thought about going out to catch a movie and wanted to see if you'd like to go, too, but it sounds like you're busy."

"I'm sorry. I'd love to, but one of my cats has a kidney infection, and I'm giving him fluids." She grinned apologetically. "Can I take a rain check?"

"Sure." Angela waved off her apology. "Some other time."

"Sounds like a plan." Ginny closed her purse with a snap and came around the counter. They walked together out of the hospital and exchanged brief farewells.

The night sky glowed with the ever-present city lights, and pedestrians hurried past closed shops and noisy nightclubs in the South Market district. Upscale warehouse conversions, now condominiums, lined Folsom Street and announced the transitional nature of this San Francisco neighborhood. The air pulsed with the thump of nightclub dance music and car stereos.

Angela waited for oncoming traffic before turning left into a parking garage. She waved her pass in front of the ticket machine, which obligingly raised the barrier, then drove in and found the assigned parking spot for her silver Toyota Prius. She climbed wearily out of the car, locked it, and took the elevator to the second floor.

As Angela opened the door to her condo, her cell phone chirped. Taking it out as she entered, she saw that the caller was her college buddy Eric Weiser. A psychiatric resident at San Francisco Central Hospital, he was virtually her only confidante and closest friend, and he had been asking her to go out with him for the last several weeks. A mixture of pleasure and guilt penetrated the fog in her mind as she answered. "Hi, Eric." She tried not to sound tired.

"Dearest Angel," Eric drawled.

"What's up?" She doffed her backpack and jacket and went into the kitchen.

"Have you had dinner yet?"

"No, I just got home."

He groaned theatrically. "Long day again, Angel?"

"Yeah. E.W.'s got a lot of patients coming in, and we're short staffed. Somebody's got to pick up the slack, and that's me." Angela opened a cabinet.

"Honey, I hear you. But listen, you've got to make time for the things you love or it'll kill you."

Angela sighed. "Yeah. I'm working on it." Failing to locate quick food in the cabinets, she opened the freezer and hunted for something to reheat. She pulled out a gourmet frozen dinner—"organic, gluten-free, low-fat"—and popped it in the microwave.

"So speaking of things you love, when're you going to go dancing at the club? I haven't seen you for weeks. I want you to meet my new boyfriend."

"Ah, maybe later this week."

"You said that last week!"

Angela heard an echo of her own complaint earlier in the day and grinned crookedly. "You're right. You know, I could use some mindless physical activity. How about I meet you there in half an hour."

"Wonderful, darling," said Eric. "I'll be waiting! Bye."

She hung up. The microwave bell rang, and Angela gingerly carried the dinner and a fork from the silverware drawer to the living room. Setting the meal down on her coffee table, she took out her phone again and checked her voice mail. There were several messages from her grandfather, George Cooper.

"Angel. Please call me back. I must speak with you," rasped his familiar voice. Angela stopped the message and erased it. The old man had been trying to reach her for over a week, but she was in no mood to talk to him. He was probably asking for money for booze, or perhaps he had another crazy story to tell her from his private stock of Romani tall tales.

Angela wolfed down her food, threw the empty tray in the trash, and went into her bedroom to change into dancing clothes. Humming happily to herself, she thumbed through her wardrobe and briefly considered black leather pants and a lacy top. Saturn's Rings had a unique goth dress code: the more exotic the clothing, the lower the entry price paid at the door. But a rebellious streak asserted itself, and she chose hip-hugger jeans and a simple black T-shirt, the minimum needed for entry into the club.

Lying on her bed, Angela pulled on the jeans and tugged them into place before getting back to her feet. The shirt went on next, and she went to her bureau to comb the tangles out of her thick black hair. Looking in the mirror, she viewed the stress circles under her eyes with dissatisfaction. She used her makeup kit to conceal them and finished with a pair of skull earrings for the sake of appearances. Whistling cheerfully, having dressed herself into the mood, she left for the club.

Saturn's Rings was a goth dancer's mecca in the city. That night, one of the more popular DJs was spinning a retro mix, and the dark, strobe-lit dance floor was crowded with a sea of moving bodies. The heavy, driving beat, growling voices, and incomprehensible lyrics combined to create an ambience that Angela had found she enjoyed. Her love of dance overcame any reticence she may have felt once, so she was at home among the goth club goers. Swaying to the rhythm, she felt the tension of the day ebbing away.

A familiar movement caught her attention. A thin platinum-blond man wearing black leather pants and a mesh shirt that revealed heavily tattooed arms was spinning in place gracefully. Angela made her way toward Eric and saw his eyes widen when he noticed her. He maneuvered among the moving bodies to meet her. They tried to talk, but in this venue, even a shout was inaudible. Eric gestured toward the wall, and they escaped to one of the alcoves there.

"Angel! You got away!" he shouted.

Angela yelled back, "Yeah. Thanks for the reminder."

"Where's that guy you were dating? Carl."

Angela shrugged eloquently. "It wasn't going anywhere."

Eric pouted. "Too bad. He was cute." He gestured to where a muscular, bare-chested man wearing black leather shorts and suspenders was dancing. "That's my gorgeous guy." He waved at the man, who acknowledged him with a smile and a wink. Then he broke his rhythm to stroll over to where they were waiting.

"Jason, meet Angela." Eric gestured elaborately at her. Jason looked her over and made a face.

"She's so straight," he complained, indicating her jeans and T-shirt.

Eric shook his head. "Angela is so not straight." He took her arm protectively. "She's got her own style. She's a rebel."

Jason grinned, stuck out his tongue, and returned to his moves, gliding smoothly among the others on the floor. Then Angela heard the music segue into a goth cover of a Don Henley hit; the singer groaned that all he wanted to do was dance.

"Let's dance," said Angela.

They moved back onto the floor, but though Angela sought for the release into trance that she usually experienced, her mind would not let go of her workday. All of the dancing shapes around her seemed distant and unreal, disconnected from her daily confrontation with the ugly underside of life. After a few minutes of self-conscious struggle to let go and move, she shook her head slightly and started to thread her way off the floor. Eric caught her eye and frowned, but then he accompanied her after shouting something at his boyfriend. She led him all the way out the front door, where she leaned against the outside wall. He dug out a pack of clove cigarettes and lit up. He gestured with the pack. "Hm?"

She shook her head. "I quit. Remember?"

He rolled his eyes and put it away then stood quietly with

Angela, smoking and staring into the night.

"It's not working," Angela said after a pause.

"What isn't working, honey?"

She kicked her heel against the wall. "I can't stop thinking about work."

"You need to keep dancing. You love to dance."

"I know. It's just..." She waved at nothing. "We could be doing so much more at the hospital, but Josef's head is so far up his ass he's looking up his own throat. He's a bureaucrat." She crossed her arms. "I've got ideas. Good ideas. But the hospital's going nowhere, and so am I."

"Go on."

"George... that's my grandfather, remember him? He's after me to start some sort of clinic. I tried, but... I'm not cut out for that. I'd very much like Josef's job, to be honest."

"You're kidding." Eric shook his head. "You'd hate being a paper pusher. You'd turn into another Josef."

"Gee, thanks," she said irritably. "Anyway, it's all I can do to keep up, and I know my skills are being wasted. Hell, Eric, sometimes I just don't know who I am anymore."

He raised a hand. "Whoa. That's deep." He took a drag on his smoke. "How does anyone know who they are, really?"

"Thank you for your analysis, but why, Dr. Freud, is your cigar so small?" Her mouth quirked into a sardonic grin.

He laughed. "It's not the size of the smoke; it's the heat of the toke." He waved the cigarette playfully, making the ash glow.

"I used to know who I was. I was raised by my grandfather, who's full-blooded Rom, and he taught me to look to my culture for my identity." Angela stared soberly up into the sky. "But I've outgrown his stories. They just don't apply to the modern world anymore."

Eric put an arm across her shoulders. "Angel, honey. Like it or not, you are the sum of everything your ancestors gave you, plus what you've got, which is plenty. Maybe you just need to figure out what your special gift is. Right?"

Angela was silent for a moment. Then she looked at him, grateful. "Yeah. Of course you're right."

He withdrew his arm and clapped his hands briskly. "Now that that's settled, let's go back in and forget about all this, okay? Dance is therapy, too."

Though she had stayed up late dancing, when Angela finally went home, she had trouble falling asleep. After finally drifting off, she dreamed of a happier time. She was at a dance party held by her gypsy relatives, and she had drunk more than her usual share of whiskey. The fiddle music swirled through the air as she danced by the campfire on the beach. A dark-haired younger man, her date for the evening, accompanied her, and he grasped her hands and whirled her through the steps of a flamenco. Then his face and form changed, and Angela found herself dancing with a young, intense, dark-haired girl she had met at that dance. She remembered the girl's name, Cassandra Grey, and she felt a new surge of excitement as they moved together. Then she glanced past the girl's shoulder and saw with every turn that there were fewer dancers. The music died, and they stopped dancing.

Cassandra stepped back, and then she was taller and a few

years older. She glared at Angela. "You killed my mother!"

Angela raised a hand in self-defense, though she felt no strong reaction, only resignation. Then, the scene changed so that she was in the Grey family's RV with her grandfather George. The girl's mother, a Rom woman in her thirties named Esmerelda Grey, was lying on the settee, with her head on the lap of her *gadjo* husband Robert. He looked helplessly up at Angela.

"She was having bad dreams, but no one could help. Then today..." He swallowed. "She collapsed, and now I can't wake her up."

Cassandra was sitting by his side, staring intently at Angela, who pulled up a cushion and kneeled on the floor next to the unconscious woman. Wind battered the sides of the vehicle, which rocked on its springs.

"Let me see what I can do," Angela said. The relief in the husband's eyes was heartbreaking. Angela had no idea how this would go, as she had never been called to perform an exorcism before. Her dream-walking ability, in which she would seem to physically enter the minds of her patients, was normally employed in more prosaic forms of therapy.

Taking a deep breath and exchanging a meaningful look with her grandfather, who sat nearby, Angela touched the woman's forehead. The light faded when she did, and a cold breath of wind shivered through the tiny space. She saw the interior of the RV blur into a forest meadow under a starry night sky. The meadow was thronged with nightmarish forms, representing the varied emotional and mental traumas that troubled the woman.

Normally, Angela would encounter one or two such creatures and, in a nonconfrontational manner, help her patient deal with them. But she realized that she could not work in her accustomed way with so many disturbances appearing at once. She recalled a promise she had made long ago, when her talent first manifested, that she would never attack anything in another's mind. But she could think of nothing else to do in this case, so she concentrated her forces. A brilliant light emanated from her body, and the shrill screams of the intrusive demons filled her mind. Then a shadow rose out of the collective bodies, and her heart clenched with fear. The Otherworld faded as she made her escape, but in her peripheral vision, she saw her grandfather lean toward her.

"Granddad, no!" Angela's dreaming self wanted to scream but could not. He touched her shoulder, and both were flung back by a soundless explosion. A blinding light dazzled her eyes, and when her sight cleared, the RV was engulfed in flames. Robert was unconscious, and the flame was burning him alive along with the young mother. Of the girl there was no trace.

The dream changed suddenly, as if the flaming RV and the dead family were swept aside by an angry hand. Angela found herself standing in a desolate landscape, and the dramatic contrast with the previous scene took her breath away. The place was strangely familiar, as if she had dreamed of it before. Rocks were strewn everywhere on the arid soil, while a reddish sky streaked with dust hung overhead. A glow on the horizon could have been sunrise or sunset; there was no way to tell. Looking down at her body, she saw that she wore an elaborate space suit.

She raised a hand to shield her eyes from the horizon and saw that she had six fingers instead of five. She drew a long, shuddering breath, and the shock woke her. But rather than lying in her bed, she found herself standing in her living room gasping for breath, her heart racing. "Shit! Not again."

Her eye was caught by a painting on the wall, illuminated by the wan moonlight, which portrayed a woman standing on a hill overlooking a beautiful valley. The woman greatly resembled Angela's dream self, and she felt relieved. The painting, a gift she received a few months ago from Roger, the patient she saw the previous day, must have triggered the dream. But the spontaneous dream-walk that left her standing in her home office was something she had not experienced in years, ever since she and her grandfather had parted ways and she had stopped using her unique talent.

She turned on the desk lamp and sat down, flipped open her laptop, and began writing in her electronic journal. The light flickered, and a gust of wind rattled the windows. She shivered and finished the write-up before returning to bed and dreamless sleep.

At the office the next morning, Angela was restless. The omnipresent paperwork was piling up again despite her best efforts to subdue it, her antiquated iMac computer had crashed and she was waiting for IT to fix it, and hospital overcrowding was rearing its ugly head again. She cradled her head in one hand, resting her elbow on the massive oak desk in her office and talking to hospital administrators on the interoffice phone.

"Just arrange the transfers," she said.

"Do you have enough doctors and nurses to handle the load?" The man's voice on the other end of the line was irritatingly matter-of-fact.

"No, we don't have the staff, but where else can they go?"

"You know, you can always arrange a county transfer."

"I'm not going to dump patients in another county, " she said.

She poked the hang-up button irritably and put the phone down. She ran her fingers through her thick, unruly black hair and rubbed her face. It had become a common, if unofficial, practice for hospitals to release some of their inpatients and put them on a one-way bus trip to the country. She would not let this hospital stoop to that practice as long as she had a say in it, but the problem remained of what to do with overfull, understaffed wards. She punched the intercom button on the desk phone again. "Ginny?"

"Yes," replied the nurse.

"Please schedule a meeting with Dr. Lindquist for me today. I'm going on my rounds shortly, so I'll check with you later this afternoon."

"Sure thing."

Later that morning, having released two patients with prescriptions, Angela was on her way to another seclusion room when she saw Josef. She waved at him. "Dr. Lindquist, got a moment?"

He saw her and strode briskly to meet her. "As a matter of fact, I was looking for you. Please walk with me to Seclusion

Room Three."

Angela raised an eyebrow but followed Josef down the crowded, noisy, echoing corridor. "I've got good news," he said.

"Am I going to get those interns I asked for?"

They stepped aside for a fast-moving nurse with a crash cart, and Josef smiled. "Even better. You've been picked to head the clinical trial you designed. You'll get the staff you need and four brand-new rTMSs."

Angela stopped walking and stared at him. "You're joking."

Josef stopped, too. "I am very serious. The folks at Radiatrics decided to assign the trial to us in order to, as they said, 'acquire legitimacy in the field.' Your groundbreaking research has attracted a lot of positive attention, so much so that our hospital was picked over several other better-staffed facilities."

"What's the catch, Josef? Here I've been asking for interns, and now all of a sudden I'm getting residents to take my place so I can run my trials. I am getting residents to take my place, right?"

Josef nodded. "Dr. Cooper, there is no catch. I've vetted the new staff already. I could not tell you anything about this until the contracts were signed. That was a stipulation."

Angela started walking again, hands in her pockets. "Okay. How about doctors to help me with the trials? I need to organize a training roster—"

Josef interrupted with a raised hand. "That's all being taken care of. The other two doctors will arrive in a couple of weeks to help you with the trial when the second batch of patients arrives. But now I want you to meet your first lucky subject."

They arrived at the seclusion room and unlocked the door.

Ginny and an orderly were waiting nearby, and they accompanied Angela and Josef.

The seclusion room was typical of its kind, being empty of all furnishings other than a gurney, but the elaborate gothic architecture above its padded walls lent it a sinister aura. Angela saw a dark-haired girl lying on the gurney, heavily sedated and restrained, and time seemed to stop for a moment. This was the girl in her dream, Cassandra Grey, somehow, miraculously, still alive. Angela felt the blood drain from her face, and she had difficulty focusing on Josef's voice.

"Dr. Cooper?"

Angela ignored him, unable to tear her eyes away from the girl. The orderly went to the gurney and stood nearby as Angela approached it.

"Dr. Cooper, this is Cassandra Grey," said Josef. "She was transferred from Lindon."

Angela licked dry lips. "How... Why is she in this seclusion room?"

Josef replied, "She was extremely agitated when she was brought in. She appears to be stabilized now."

Cassandra turned her head and looked at Angela. Her eyes widened, and though she was heavily sedated, she opened her mouth to try to speak. However, a coughing fit shook her slight frame. Ginny went to her side and eased an arm behind her shoulders to help her.

Angela's mind was racing, but she kept all expression from her face. She could not risk Cassandra revealing her past. If word got out that she had been a psychic healer, her credibility as a psychiatrist would be destroyed, and she might very well face criminal charges because she had fled the scene of the fire that took the lives of the Grey family. She shook her head. "I don't think she's a good candidate for the trial. She's too young."

Josef frowned. "We needed a young female patient, presenting with schizophrenic tendencies, and Ms. Grey has been prescreened. As of now she's eligible for this trial."

Angela took a deep breath to calm herself. Cassandra looked over the nurse's shoulder and met Angela's gaze, and her dark eyes were accusatory.

Josef continued. "The clinical protocol specifically excludes the treating physician from choosing patients for evaluation. You know that."

Angela decided that the safest course of action was to talk to Cassandra alone and try to salvage the situation. Perhaps she could persuade the girl to stay quiet. Though it was unlikely that anyone would take her seriously in her current condition, she could offer devastating testimony against Angela when she was stabilized.

Addressing the orderly, Angela said, "Transfer Cassandra to a seclusion room with a mattress. I'll be there right after lunch."

She turned to Josef. "If I find in my evaluation that she's unfit for the trial, I reserve the right to reject her."

"That's your prerogative. I expect a full report on this patient."

Angela noticed that Cassandra had fallen unconscious. She accompanied Josef out of the room.

The Pit

A bottomless pit opened and
I fell in, and fell and fell
Voices from far above
Ask me who I am, what I am
Why do they care? I've fallen.

This is rest, this is peace,
To fall forever, no bottom, no end,
Farther from the light and freedom
Freedom to die? Freedom to live?
Why do I care? I've fallen.
- C

3.

After lunch, Angela and Ginny walked together, through the corridor bustling with interns and orderlies, toward Cassandra's seclusion room.

Ginny consulted her notes. "What's the schedule for Cassandra?"

"I'll evaluate her for the trial, and if she is eligible, we'll move her to a treatment room to get her stabilized." Angela flipped the paper back on her clipboard, dodging a trotting intern. She was inclined to find some pretext for transferring Cassandra back to Lindon to prevent her from exposing Angela's past.

They arrived at the seclusion room door and paused. Angela looked for the security personnel that usually accompanied her when first visiting violent patients. "Where are the HPs?"

"Give 'em a few minutes. They've got a live one in admitting."

Angela sighed and unlocked the door. "Give me half an hour." Picking up one of the chairs from the hallway, she carried it into the room. Watery gray daylight filtered through the barred window of the room, illuminating the single mattress that was its sole furniture. Unlike most seclusion room windows, this one was low enough to provide a view of the grounds.

Cassandra was sitting cross-legged in the center of the mattress, and next to her was a stack of paper and a large blunt crayon. Angela set down her chair but remained standing. The teenager stared at Angela with an abstract intensity, as if waiting for the first move in an elaborate game. Angela was silent for a moment, heart racing, her resolve already evaporating. "Cassandra? Is that really you?" she finally asked.

"Yes." Cassandra's reply was flat.

"I thought you died in the fire! God, I..." Angela felt her throat catch.

In the same inflectionless voice, Cassandra asked, "Did you bother to look for me? I remember that you and the old sorcerer ran off."

Angela sat heavily in the chair. "That was my grandfather. But it was so long ago. Where have you been all this time?"

Cassandra waved vaguely. "On the street. I had no choice. It was that or—well, here."

"I'm so sorry. Everything was so chaotic, and then when they found those bodies..." She winced. Those bodies had been Cassandra's family.

Cassandra stared at Angela. "You owe me, Angela Cooper. I want you to protect me from it. From them."

Angela frowned. "From whom?"

"The voices. The ghosts. The shadow. Whatever it is. I know you want to send me back to Lindon, but I've got you over a barrel and you know it."

Angela stood abruptly. "You can't do that. I'll lose everything."

Cassandra shrugged. "I lost everything because of you. You've got to fix it." She turned and rolled onto her belly, crossed her arms under her chin, and stared at the wall.

Angela started pacing, picking her teeth. "You know, I left all that behind after that night. I'm a respectable psychiatrist now. I don't play mind tricks anymore."

Cassandra slapped her hand on the mattress. She looked over her shoulder and glared at Angela. "The shadow is right here! In this room. Right now. It killed my mom and dad and sisters, and now it's going to kill me and you. So you'd better play those mind tricks again or..." She made an expressive throat-cutting gesture then rolled back over on her back and stared at the ceiling.

"There's nothing in this room. No one else at all."

Cassandra propped herself up on one elbow. "Really? How's your granddad these days, Doc?"

Angela was confused. "What?"

"It will get your family if it doesn't get you first," said Cassandra. Her face contorted. "Oh God, no." She curled up into a fetal position and started rocking and moaning.

"It's okay. You don't need to go there right now. Breathe." Angela resisted the urge to move closer, in case Cassandra went into convulsions.

Cassandra sat up and looked down at her hands. "It's... it's going to kill again." She looked up at Angela, all anger gone, a pleading expression on her face. "Please, you've got to stop it."

Outside the hospital, a woman on a cell phone call stopped talking abruptly and in a toneless voice said, "Before I take you for myself."

A homeless man nearby said, "Give yourself to me."

A businessman on his cell phone said, "Why do you resist?" He clutched his skull. "Man, this headache is killing me."

Cassandra yelled, "Get out of my head! No!"

"Where are those HPs? Cassandra, focus on my voice. Listen."

Cassandra rolled to her feet and turned to look out of the security-screened window. She pointed outside. "He's next!"

Angela reached out to Cassandra. "Cassie, calm down! I'm going to—"

Cassandra whirled, backing away. Her eyes were fierce and piercing. "Don't touch me."

Angela lowered her hand and tried to inject soothing tones into her voice. "Cassandra, I'm not your enemy."

"It's here, and it wants to show you something." Cassandra's voice was once again emotionless. Angela relaxed minutely but knew that the episode wasn't over yet.

"No one else is in here. Are you talking about your voices?" she said.

Cassandra pointed out of the window. "He had a gift, too. Now he's going to die."

Angela looked at where Cassandra was pointing. She saw a man, dressed in a formal suit, sitting on a bench directly across the lawn from the window. It was Roger, her psychotherapy patient whom she had released the day before. What was he doing here so soon? "Roger?"

Roger stared back at Angela as though he saw her. He dipped his hand into his jacket pocket and raised it to his head. He was holding a pistol. Time slowed to a crawl. Angela lurched on leaden feet toward the window, her hand out, and shouted, "No!"

There was a popping sound. Roger's body jerked, and he collapsed to the sidewalk.

George sat with his back to the mast of his live-aboard sailing yacht, nursing a can of generic beer. He lazily scanned the boat, noting with only a tremor of dismay that the deck was filthy with bird droppings. The lines were in disarray, and the brightly colored mainsail was still piled up in its web of lazy jacks, salt stained and faded by the sun. He silently promised himself that he would clean it up after he finished his beer.

He had built his vessel years before when he had been at his peak in the business of creating handmade, one-of-a-kind wooden boats for discerning enthusiasts, and it had been a showcase for his best work. From the polished rails of the bow pulpit, through the hand-rubbed cedar deck planking, the engraved brass portholes, and the elaborate teak finishing trim, to the name, "Gypsy Angel"—complete with a stylized dancing, winged Rom woman—painted on the stern, this boat had been a peacock among the blank white pigeons of the other sailboats. Neglect had robbed his masterwork of its former glory, and the guilt sometimes weighed on him.

Taking one last pull from the can, he crumpled it in a massive fist and tossed it into the cockpit a few feet away. Using the topping lift that ran down from the masthead, he hauled himself to his feet and, grasping the boom, made his way unsteadily to where the companionway led below decks. Suddenly, he felt a chill run down his spine. He stopped, startled, and glanced around him. All seemed normal, but then another chill made him shiver. He noticed that the afternoon light appeared to be dimming rapidly. He swore sulfurously at the cloudless sky. Closing his eyes, he attempted to ignore the pounding headache as he opened his inner sight. A scene of his granddaughter screaming flickered in his mind, and a faint popping came to his ears. "Angel!" He scrambled into the cockpit and swung down the companionway, banging his elbows painfully in the process. He swore again and lunged for his phone. With shaking fingers, he punched Angela's office number.

He waited impatiently for the phone to ring and then heard her outgoing office message. "This is Doctor Cooper's office. If this is a medical emergency, please hang up and dial 9-1-1. Otherwise, stay on the line and, at the beep, please leave your name, number, and a brief message, and I will get back to you as soon as I can."

He waited for the beep. "Angel, this is your grandfather. Please pick up." He paused. "Okay, please call me. Please." He punched the off button, set the phone down, and rubbed his aching elbow. He groaned as he surveyed the sty that he had made of his floating home. His head swam.

"Who do you think you are, George? You cannot help your-self, and you cannot help Angela." Filled with a familiar sense of self-loathing, he staggered to the master cabin. He told himself he would sleep off his latest binge and do some house cleaning, and then maybe he could take a much-needed shower and visit Angela at her hospital. Maybe he could make her a charm. If he really tried, he could make her see that she needed him. Reassured, he collapsed on the stained mattress and passed out.

Paramedics were loading a body bag into the ambulance. Josef and Angela conferred with the police nearby. Onlookers were gawking beyond the police tape, and a group of journalists and cameramen were jockeying for position.

"Officer, thank you," said Josef. "We'll send someone to the morgue later to assist with the report."

"Much appreciated, Doctor." The police officer retrieved a clipboard from Lindquist.

Angela was numb. "He checked out yesterday. He promised to stay on the meds."

Josef took her by the arm and stepped away from the crowd. "What about the other patient, the girl? You said she knew what was going on."

Angela shook her head. "She pointed out the window at him and told me..." She paused until she could continue. "She told me that he would die."

The ambulance pulled away, and the police began cleaning up the scene. One of the hospital staff was speaking to the journalists, and Angela hoped that the story wouldn't further blacken the hospital's already dubious reputation.

"That makes no sense. She must have seen him outside and wanted to make a dramatic point," said Josef.

Angela sighed. "Probably."

Josef put a hand on Angela's shoulder. "Listen, I can send someone else to the morgue. You don't have to go."

"No, he was my patient. I can do this." She would mourn Roger later, but there was business to attend to first.

They began walking back to the hospital. The rest of the day was a blur for Angela. Later, when she left to go across town to the morgue, she remembered the compassionate looks of her coworkers, particularly Ginny, but she could not remember the details of her workday.

Angela shivered in the cold of the morgue. Occupying the center of the room was the autopsy slab where Roger's sheet-covered body lay under stark, blank illumination. The horror of his death was simultaneously magnified and diminished by the sterile setting. The coroner pulled back a corner of the sheet to reveal his face, and Angela felt a lurch in her gut when she saw the ugly gunshot wound. She nodded. "Roger Charles." Her voice was miraculously steady. "Medicated for bipolar disorder with psychotic tendencies. He was just discharged yesterday."

The coroner read from the death certificate. "Roger Charles, white male, age thirty-six. Death by self-inflicted gunshot wound." His pen scribbled for a moment, and then he covered Roger's face.

Angela bowed her head briefly. "Can I stay here a moment?"

"Sure." He stripped his gloves, picked up his clipboard, and left. Angela remained standing quietly, looking down at the sheet that silhouetted the form of her patient and friend.

"What the hell, Roger?" She reached out to touch the sheet.

His initial seventy-two-hour treatment and release had occurred several months earlier, after a violent altercation with one of his critics. He had asked for follow-up therapeutic counseling and had become one of the only patients with whom she could practice talk therapy. He had insisted on coming to her instead of going to a less expensive therapist. Since he could afford the sessions, he got what he wanted.

Memories of the many hours he spent in her office came flooding back, particularly the session in which he had broken through his repressed emotions and had begun his road to recovery. She had led him to confront his voices, voices that tormented him and, he had said, made him do degrading things to himself. The voices were like a bomb ticking away in his unconscious, and when the bomb finally exploded into emotion, Angela was ready. "It's okay. Let it out." She sat at the edge of her seat, facing Roger, who was curled up in a fetal position on the couch and sobbing uncontrollably.

"She was my life. I left her and the kids. And they... they died." His muffled voice was cracked and raw, far different from the confident baritone of the successful artist who had come to her a year before.

"It wasn't your fault, Roger," said Angela. "It was the drunk driver who killed them, not you."

Roger wailed and reached blindly to Angela. She hesitated and then grasped his hands with hers as he pulled her toward him. She ended up on her knees at the couch, and she laid her hand on his shoulder.

After his breakthrough, his disorder had lost much of its power over him, and he was able to begin the process of healing. He grew happier, with real confidence rather than the braggadocio of the past. Near the end, he had come to terms with his attraction to Angela and realized that it could not lead to anything. He gracefully acceded to reality, another indication of his recovery, but he stubbornly refused to consider her as just his therapist. One day he presented her with a princely gift, an original painting that would have fetched tens of thousands of dollars at the national galleries.

When he handed her the wrapped package, Angela was deeply moved. "Roger, you know I can't accept presents."

He held the package in his outstretched hands. "Doc, I know. Please. Take it anyway."

Angela hesitated. Then she took the package and tore away the paper. As she was expecting, it was a painting.

"Roger, it's beautiful!" She smiled at him, genuinely pleased. He returned her smile.

He said, "I thought you'd like it. It came to me in a dream. It would make my day if you'd ignore the rules just this once."

Angela shook her head. "Just between me and you, then. I'll take it home. I know exactly where to hang it."

It was truly a painting to inspire dreams. And now it was her only link to a man with whom she had shared a connection that transcended the usual doctor-patient relationship. Her memories of him were overlaid with the pain of failure.

Angela fingered the morgue sheet, pulling back a corner to reveal the uninjured part of Roger's face. "I'm so sorry." Her tears dampened the sheet. Then, hesitantly, she touched Roger's brow. A whisper came and went, and she looked around at the otherwise empty morgue. "Who's there?"

The whispering grew louder and sounded odd, as if multiple voices were speaking simultaneously. The words were unintelligible. Then, a shadow obscured Roger's face, and when it cleared, he looked different, angular and lean, and his eyes were open and staring at Angela. She jerked her hand back in shock. Angela backed away from the slab, saw movement out of the corner of her eye, and looked up. The walls of the room had vanished, revealing a night sky above and walls of intense darkness all around. Angela felt her breath quicken. "Oh no. Not here!"

Angela backed farther away from the morgue slab with the corpse. She stumbled but caught her balance. "Okay. I can get out of here," she muttered. "Where's the trail?" She circled the slab, peering at the uncertain ground. Meanwhile, the sound had grown into the muttering roar of a crowd, emanating from the trees. Angela accelerated her search.

"Ha!" She darted over to what appeared to be a row of floor tiles, connected to the slab, that were embedded in the otherwise black, indistinct ground. She stepped onto the tiles and glanced over her shoulder. A vast, inky cloud of darkness occluded the stars above the forest. Angela stifled a whimper and forced herself to walk slowly along the tiles, feeling a tingling between her shoulder blades. A light arose, and the walls of the examination room appeared around her, first as a ghostly overlay on the dark forest and then gradually taking on solidity. Moments later, she had returned to the room, all signs of the Otherworld gone. Angela found a chair and collapsed into it, sweating. Silence reigned. She buried her face in her hands.

Angela shivered. What the hell was that about? After a moment, she rose unsteadily, staring at the now-normal corpse of Roger, and left the room. She was tempted to take the rest of the day off, but she knew there was too much work waiting, and she didn't want to foist it off on her colleagues. With a herculean effort, she pushed what had just happened out of her mind.

The rest of the day passed in a blur, and when her shift was over, Angela left for home without checking on Cassandra, who had been sedated after Roger's suicide. Angela could not bring herself to think about Cassandra or the morgue, but when she got home, there was a message from Eric. "I heard on the grapevine what happened today. Honey, I'm coming over, and I'm bringing my two friends, Jack Daniels and Jim Beam. Bye."

She dropped her purse on the floor by the couch and collapsed into it. Angela could not stop replaying the horrifying morgue scene in her mind. What was that shadow, and what had caused the vision of that strange face to overlay Roger's features? Whatever it was, she had never seen anything like it in any of her dream-walking sessions.

The security buzzer jostled her from her reverie, and she went to the intercom.

"It's three bad boys, hon." Eric's voice was light, and Angela felt giddy with relief that she would not need to be alone for at least a few hours. She buzzed him into the gate.

Moments later she answered his knock at the door. Wafting in through the door was an amazing aroma of pizza, and Angela could not help smiling upon seeing her friend's face over the enormous box. "God, I forgot I was hungry." Her stomach grumbled.

"Beware of shrinks bearing gifts," he intoned as she relieved him of his burden. He followed her into her living room with a paper sack, set it down, and removed two bottles of whiskey with a flourish. "Jim, Jack, this is my friend Angela. She's going to wrap her lips around you and suck you dry."

Angela laughed, feeling her tension begin to melt away as she went to the kitchen to fetch glasses. When she returned, the box was already open, and Eric was standing by the stereo. Angela set the tumblers down.

"I'm in the mood for some Serenaders," he announced.

"Sounds great." Angela poured two double shots and sat down in front of the pizza. The sounds of retro string music further banished her black mood as Eric sat down next to her and lifted his tumbler.

"To friends," he said, and they clinked their glasses. Angela tossed back a gulp and immediately coughed, tears streaming down her cheeks. He patted her back. "Careful, hon; Jim's a rough character."

Angela set the tumbler down and picked up a slice of pizza. Biting into it, she closed her eyes and relished the flavor. They ate together in silence for a few minutes, enjoying the music. Angela paused mid-slice. She picked up her drink again and sipped; Eric watched her sidelong as he ate. She turned to look at him, and his eyes filled with pity.

"He was going to be okay." That was all she could say, as her shoulders heaved and she sobbed helplessly. Eric wrapped his arms around her and rocked, murmuring nonsense words.

When she took a deep breath, he released her, held her shoulders, and looked at her. "Are you okay?"

Angela nodded and dabbed at her eyes with a tissue. She sat back on the couch and sighed heavily. "I'm sorry."

Eric shook his head. "Nuh-uh, sister. That was a shocker for anyone. You get to cry all you want."

Angela got up and started pacing. "I keep telling myself that there wasn't anything I could do, but it's hard to believe. He was suicidal when he first came to me, after all."

Eric poured more whiskey and held out the glass. Angela took it and tossed it back, this time without coughing.

"Thanks." She stopped and looked inquiringly at Eric. "Can you keep a secret?"

Eric nodded. "Can I ever. Try me."

She looked away and then faced him again. "Cassandra, my new patient, knew that Roger was going to kill himself."

Eric opened his mouth, but Angela interrupted him before he could speak. "No, let me finish. She began exhibiting what looked like a schizoid break, claiming to hear voices. Then she turned and pointed out the window and said that he was going to die." She picked at her teeth. "I looked, and there was Roger. He seemed to see me through the window, and then he shot himself." Angela tried to keep her voice steady. Eric was silent, and she started fidgeting again.

Finally, Eric spoke up. "Angel, I believe you. But what do you think it means?"

She looked down at her hands then glanced back at Eric. "I know this is going to sound crazy, but it's possible she's psychic."

Eric was incredulous. "Okay, that's a little bit more than I expected."

"I know." She came back and sat down on the couch. "That's what I want you to keep secret. You know psychism is not a popular idea in the profession. I told Josef what she said, and he dismissed it."

Eric chose another slice of pizza. "If she were psychic..." He raised his hands. "I'm not saying she is, but if she were, then maybe these voices she hears aren't just in her head."

Angela eyed him. "I wasn't going to say that." She lifted her unfinished slice of pizza and started eating. "But I don't think I can dismiss her like Josef did." They ate in silence for a moment. Then Angela said, "I needed to tell someone about her." She looked at Eric. "Do you think I'm losing it?"

He grinned. "Of course you're losing it. That doesn't make you any crazier than the rest of us." He hugged her with his right arm and shook her gently. "You can trust me, Angel. Lips are sealed."

They ate the rest of the pizza and listened to music for a while, and then Eric, satisfied that Angela was over the worst of her shock, left for home.

Cassandra awoke in a cold sweat, staring at the ceiling. Her dreams had been chaotic and were already fading from her memory. For a moment, she struggled to free herself from the soaked sheets that had wound around her body, but then she relaxed, motionless, remembering the day before. The voices had warned her that Angela would not listen to her, and she had wanted to lash out at the doctor. But when she had seen Angela's face after Roger shot himself, she had felt a pang of sympathy and an unexpected surge of protectiveness toward the doctor.

The effort of fending off the onslaught of the dark one who commanded the voices had exhausted her, so when the nurse came with the sedative, she had surrendered to the warm darkness of unconsciousness. Now, awake again, she was filled with anger at how Angela had abandoned her after the fire. That was when the voices had started, and they drove her from place to place, controlling her choices and overshadowing everything. Her life since then had been a living hell, and she was determined that Angela should make it right once again. She was certain Angela had the power to do so.

Cassandra considered pressing the call button to ask the nurse for more sedative. Though the aftereffects of nausea and low-grade headaches were unpleasant, anything was preferable to the whiplash of the dark one and his minions. But she could not quite rouse herself enough to reach up to the wall above her head, so she lay there, staring upward, feeling the sweat drying on her body and the chill of the damp sheets.

After a while, she felt the sense of calm urgency that usually preceded the arrival of a poem. With a resigned sigh, she reached over and flipped on the light switch. Picking up the pad of paper by her bedside, she held the pen for a moment then started writing. The poems often flowed smoothly when the voices were quiet—like they were now—and soon the short piece was complete. She reread it to make sure it said what she had felt and set the pad back down. Then it hit her: she should write poetry for Angela. Surely, if she did well, Angela would consider her as more than a sick girl and take her seriously. With renewed enthusiasm she began another poem, addressing a topic that she was sure Angela would understand. This one went more slowly, and while she was considering the last stanza, the whispering began. Cassandra paused in her writing, unable to finish the poem. She could not stop herself from moaning, once again feeling the sinking sensation of defeat before the dark one.

Remembering the call button, she slapped her hand against it just before the voices drowned her consciousness, and then she curled up into a fetal position. She was dimly aware of a white-clad form entering the room. Blessed darkness soon arrived, and with the last shred of her awareness, she felt gratitude that, at last, someone had silenced the voices.

Wednesday morning, Angela entered the hospital foyer and stopped, staring. An elderly, powerfully built man, white-bearded and bushy browed, wearing a cap, faded Hawaiian shirt, and dingy jeans, rose from one of the chairs.

"Granddad? What are you doing here? I told you not to—"

He raised his hand. "I know, but you do not return my calls, and we must speak." George spoke with a thick accent despite having lived most of his life in the States.

Angela glanced around the room and pitched her voice so only he could hear. "Did anyone see you come in?"

He waved his hand vaguely. "You know I can come and go without being seen. I taught you that trick!"

Angela grabbed George by the elbow. "Okay. In here." She steered him into one of the interview rooms and shut the door behind them. She rounded on him. "What's going on? Why'd you come here?"

"That is no way to speak to your grandfather, Angel."

She pointed her finger at him. "You know the rules. No visiting me at work. What do you want, anyway? Money for booze?"

George found a chair and sat heavily. He lowered his face

into his hands for a moment, apparently exhausted. Angela's anger gave way to concern, though she suspected he was up to his usual manipulative tricks. "Granddad?"

He looked up. His face was drawn. "There is a shadow stalking you. I cannot sleep for the horror of it."

"I..." She stared at him. "I told you never to go there with me anymore. Ever."

George took out a preloaded pipe and pulled a lighter out of the same pocket. "You cannot abandon your past, Angel."

Angela took the pipe out of his hand. "No smoking. Yes, I can, and I did. I'm a professional psychiatrist and—"

His voice echoed in her mind. *You are a healer. I trained you.*

"Don't start with that now." She felt anger rising again. "No mind tricks."

George stared at her, his eyes glittering. "You smell like the Otherworld. Have you been dream-walking?"

"I don't know what you're talking about." Angela forced herself to return his stare. "I won't be browbeaten by you."

"Okay." He fumbled in another pocket. "I made something for you." He proffered a small, embroidered bag.

Angela crossed her arms. "No charms. Are you even listening to me?"

"Your heart is a Romani heart," George declared. "Yes, you are also half gadjo, it is true, but the heart of the Roma is stronger than anything that beats in the chest of the gadjo. I taught you to see that."

Angela raised her voice to match his. "Granddad, I saw a family hurt by you, and I was declared *marimé* because of it. Nana herself condemned both of us! Your sister!" She didn't need this argument, and the blood pounding in her temples promised another headache.

"What she did, she did for the family," said George. "But I stayed with you, Angel."

"Of course you did. Who else was going to pay your slip fees after you quit working?" She regretted saying it the moment the words came out of her mouth, and she saw the hurt in George's face as his hands clenched and unclenched. Then, with a visible effort, he relaxed his hands.

"I am grateful to you, Granddaughter. I lost my way after that night."

Angela crossed her arms. "I had everything under control. You shouldn't have been there, and that family was killed. Except..."

George pounced on her hesitation. "Except what? I know you are hiding something from me."

Angela threw up her hands, exasperated. "Look, I know you care about me, but I have patients who need my skill as a psychiatrist, not as a crazy, half-gypsy witch."

"Angel, listen to me." George's voice was gentle again. "Even if you do not want my help, even if you are hiding something, you are in danger. Please, please be careful."

George left the room, looking shrunken and old. Angela felt the familiar anguish but could not trust herself to speak. After a moment, she went to the door to look for him, but he was nowhere to be seen.

She stood silently, thinking. Despite his urging, she couldn't go back to her old healing ways. It was just too dangerous. Even if she did, she could not forgive George for the part he played in the deaths of those people. Nevertheless, he was the only family she had in the world now that she was outcast from the Roma. No one else would understand her secret past or the talent that had marked her since childhood. Angela felt a lump in her throat and fought back tears. She had work to do, and this was no time to fall apart.

She took a deep breath. It was time to check on Cassandra. Her new patient had been moved to a regular hospital room and kept under sedation after her episode the previous day.

Angela quietly entered the treatment room. The nurse in attendance was there, checking Cassandra's vitals.

"What her status?" Angela took the chart from its hook at the end of the bed.

"She's stable now, but I had to use benzo." The nurse shook her head. "This is the third antipsychotic we've tried. Her heart rate spiked at well over 180 for ten minutes."

Angela flipped through the chart. "Clozapine, olanzapine, and now lithium?" Angela closed the chart and hung it back up, thinking hard. She knew there was something more than a simple psychotic break at work, and her instincts told her she would need to overcome her reluctance to face Cassandra if she wanted to learn more. "Thank you, nurse. Let's take her off the Lactated Ringer's tomorrow morning. Keep her on benzo as needed, but cut the dosage back. I want her mildly sedated." She examined Cassandra's eyes and felt her pulse.

"Yes, Doctor," said the nurse.

Angela stood quietly for a moment. A decision needed to be made here. If she declined to treat Cassandra, the girl would be transferred back to Lindon, doubtless to be bused away to a rural county to end up homeless and, probably, come to an unfortunate end. She looked at the nurse.

"I want her transferred to Room 325," Angela said. "I'm going to personally prep her for the clinical trial."

Angela left the room to continue her rounds.

DUST TO DUST

Dust mote, drifting light
Forever seeking the earth
Trade places with me
- C

SUPER HERO

You thought you could fly
I thought so too
Save my world, just try
I said to you

You rode on the wind
Like a young witch
Your mission, to mend
A soul restitch

But shadows arose
And struck you down
Death came to oppose
Your
- C (unfinished)

4.

AFTER GEORGE left the hospital, he relaxed his concentration, dispelling the glamour of invisibility with unaccustomed difficulty. He returned to his car, a fifties vintage Cadillac in a sad state of repair, and after paying the parking garage, drove back home to the marina.

The night before, he had dreamed that Angela was walking in the clouds above the night-blanketed earth, shining with her own light, and each footstep was accompanied by the muted rumble of thunder. Behind her was a vast, dark cloud, a shadow filled with malevolence that chilled him and made him sit bolt upright and shout a warning to her.

She had no idea what effect she had on the world when she dream-walked. To her, it was a simple gift of psychic ability, and she dismissed the experiences she had had as a child when she would spontaneously dream-walk and awaken far from home, shivering in the night.

George pulled up to the marina and parked. He let himself in through the gate that opened onto the pier where his live-aboard sailboat was docked. His neighbor, who was washing a forty-foot cruising sloop, waved in greeting. "Hey, George. I'm having some friends over to watch the game over some brews this afternoon. Care to join us?"

George smiled and shook his head. "Not tonight, Paul. Maybe another time?"

"Sure thing. You know, it's been a while since we've all sailed together. Maybe we'll organize a flotilla, go to Catalina sometime."

"That sounds like a very good idea." He clambered aboard his wooden yacht as his neighbor chuckled and bent back to his cleaning. George looked at his own boat, which suffered in comparison because he had not kept his promise to himself to do his own house cleaning. Sighing, he continued belowdecks.

The first thing George decided to do was to contact his allies. Angela refused his help, so he decided that he would help her through the agency of others. He would see if any of his old friends and family members would set up a watch and keep an eye on her at the hospital as she came and went. He decided to start with the son of one of his cousins, a man named Riley, who had at one time worked as a bookie at the Golden Gate Fields horse racing track in Oakland.

After checking his tattered phone book, he placed a quick call and confirmed that his cousin's son still worked there. He locked the boat, walked back to his car, and drove to the track, hoping that after all this time he would still find a warm reception. He negotiated the freeway, grumbling as he tried to recall the correct lanes and exits in the concrete maze of the East Bay area. He breathed a sigh of relief when he pulled into the parking lot.

George got out and made his way to the club entrance, where he expected to be able to meet Riley. He presented an old business card—*George Cooper, Boatbuilder, Esq.*—and waited in the entryway. Soon, a familiar face and form emerged from the building and caught him in a bear hug.

"Georgie! What a surprise!" The younger man bussed him

on each cheek, held his shoulders, and looked him up and down. "You haven't changed a bit, old man!"

George saw that Riley had put on some weight since he last saw him but didn't mention this. "Riley! You look very well. How is the racing business?"

"It's got its ups and down. Come on in. I've got a table." They went into the club, catching each other up on minutiae. They sat at a table by a window that provided a view onto the track.

"So, George, I guess you're not here to bet on the horses."

George shook his head. "No. I need your help." George explained what Angela had been doing, keeping it brief and not mentioning his own excursions into the world of spirits. "She and I are still not speaking," he concluded sadly. "And so I hope that somebody else can do what I am not allowed to do: keep an eye on my Angel."

Riley's face had grown serious as he listened to George. He shook his head. "She has been declared marimé. We can't talk to her or even acknowledge her." He shifted in his seat. "George, the world moves on, but our people, our family, do not. She has a talent, and that talent got her in deep trouble with the family. I don't want to abandon her to her fate, but my hands are tied."

George's heart sank. "This is our Angela. Her life is in danger. Does that mean nothing to you?"

Riley raised his hand. "I'm on your side, George. But I already know what the family is going to say. Anyway, you know they don't really listen to me. I'm half outcast already, what with my gadjo wife and all."

George smacked the table with his fist and stood, looming over the table. "You're not even going to try!"

Riley stood as well. "George, you know me! I've already tried over and over to make them reverse their decision. They don't even acknowledge Angela exists anymore." Riley's expression was anguished and his fists clenched.

Several of the other patrons stared at the two men in alarm, and the maître d' was signaling to the waitstaff. George noticed this and scowled. "I need to go. There is no help or honor with the Roma now." He turned and left, pushing his way past the other tables.

George went back to the car to sit while his anger cooled enough for him to drive. He really needed a drink, but he knew he could not have another one while Angela was in danger. He fumed over the declaration of marimé, or "unclean," that had been placed over him and Angela. At the time, he had been in shock over the death of those people and overwhelmed with guilt, and since then he had numbed his pain with drink, but now something from the old world, his world, threatened his only grandchild. He felt galvanized into action.

A thought occurred to him. He knew that Angela had friends who worked with her. Perhaps one of them would look after his granddaughter, but he had no way to reach them, not having their phone numbers. However, Angela would have her friends' numbers in a phone book at her condo. He was sure of it.

Starting his car, George drove away.

George stood at the door to Angela's condo, sorting through the keys on his key chain. Finding the correct one, he inserted it into the lock, mumbling a fervent prayer that she hadn't changed her locks since she had given him this key some years before.

The key turned, and he went in. There was plenty of daylight from the large windows opposite the front door. He began his methodical search in the kitchen. Within moments, he found a black book in one of the drawers and thanked the spirits that she had not trusted all of her information to her smart phone. He paused, feeling a pang of guilt at violating Angela's privacy, but then he started flipping through it. None of the names looked familiar until he got to the Es. He recognized the name of her friend, Eric Weiser.

"Ah, the gay man," he muttered. He frowned, thinking of the friends she had that he never really liked. Eric topped the list, but he knew that Angela and Eric were very close. Recognizing that his prejudice could further endanger his granddaughter, he shrugged it off with an effort. George glanced around the kitchen for a phone and then hesitated. "No, no, don't call from her own house, you old fool." After jotting down the number on a scratch pad and taking the piece of paper, he closed the book and carefully replaced it where he had found it. Letting himself out of the house, George started home.

As George approached his boat, he heard his phone ringing and hurried to climb aboard. He clambered hastily down the companionway and grabbed the receiver. "Hello! Hello!"

"Georgie," said Riley. "Please don't hang up. I need to tell you something."

George scowled, disappointed that it wasn't Angela and that it was his intransigent relative. "Okay, say what you will say."

"Your sister, Nadia..."

"She declared marimé on us both!"

"Yeah, I know. But word is that she regrets it. I know you and she haven't been on speaking terms."

"*Amria!*" George smacked the bulkhead.

"Hey, tone it down. Look, if you're man enough, you'll talk to Nadia. If you can get that marimé reversed, you'll have Roma swarming all over your girl's problems. Got that?"

George was red faced and breathing heavily. "I got that. Okay. I will hang up now." He punched the off button, muttering curses. He would be damned if he would reach out to the old broad. With renewed determination, he dug the slip of paper out of his pocket and dialed Eric's number. The phone rang twice, and then a young man's voice answered. "George?"

George looked at the phone. "How did you...? Oh yes, the caller ID thing. Eric, yes, this is Angela's grandfather."

Eric chuckled. "Angela told me you didn't have a cell phone." He paused. "Of course, this is about her, isn't it?"

"Yes, it is. I am very worried about her." He cleared his throat uncomfortably.

"Me, too." There was another awkward pause.

"Please tell me what is happening," George said.

"It's kinda complicated. I think we'd better talk face-to-face. Say, want to grab a bite of breakfast tomorrow, my treat? We can talk then."

George shifted uncomfortably. He was ready to admit that

he was very old-fashioned and he was still uncomfortable with gay men. However, he would do anything to help Angela. "Yes, that is good. Can we meet at the North Beach Cafe at nine?"

"Sure, that works for me. See you then." Eric hung up, and George held onto the receiver for a moment, staring into the distance.

"My Angel. What are you doing now?" He felt a sinking sensation in the pit of his stomach. As if the air had thinned, he had difficulty breathing, and the shadows of the evening were thick and filled with menace. There was clearly a supernatural element of danger, and he knew what he had to do next.

George used the head and then went into the master cabin. Rummaging through several ornately carved boxes, he pulled out an elaborately embroidered cloth, a box, and a small pouch. He made his way back to the dining salon, laid out the cloth on the table, and sat. "Let us see about you, mister shadow." It had been years since he had even read the cards, but he decided that he had to know what was happening. Opening the box, he pulled out a worn deck of tarot cards and set them down. Next, he opened the pouch and pulled out a necklace with a cloth bag for a pendant and slipped it over his head. While clumsily shuffling the cards, he allowed his mind to become still, relaxing his body and emptying himself of the day's concerns. Then, humming a tune, he closed his eyes and began rocking in place, casting his mind into the Otherworld.

"Guardian, friend, attend me now," he chanted in Romani. He felt himself settle into trance as he rocked and, with rapid flicks of his fingers, dealt eight of the cards in a wheel pattern and placed his fingers in the center of the wheel. A tingling sensation at the nape of his neck spread rapidly across his shoulders, and he knew his Guardian was present. Silently welcoming the spirit and apologizing for his long absence from the work, he opened his eyes and examined the cards. He drew a hissing breath at what he saw.

At the point farthest from him on the wheel, the ten of Swords was flanked by Death and the Tower. He knew that when this trio of cards appeared together they indicated mortal danger. But what disturbed him most was the inverted Fool on the left of that trio, followed by the eight of Wands, and at the point nearest him, the inverted Lovers. Both he and Angela were endangered by something, perhaps a ghost or spirit, and it had a powerful connection with Angela.

Looking to the right, he saw that the descending cards were the two of Cups and the Hanged Man. He sighed heavily. His granddaughter, he knew, had had no luck in the arena of love, and according to this reading, she would be betrayed by one for whom she cared deeply.

He closed his eyes again and resumed his chanting and rocking. He slipped further into trance and placed himself into an alert, questioning, but undistracted frame of mind. He sought a vision of what he should do. The void within his emptied mind continued to shift and swirl with random shapes of color, but no images presented themselves. He waited for what felt like an eternity, but then his back pain flared up, distracting him and breaking his concentration. With an explosive breath, he opened his eyes and stretched, his back crackling. He saw that it was night already, and since he had not turned on a light, the boat was pitch black. Feeling his way confidently, he flicked on a switch, doffed the necklace, and stowed it and his cards in his trunk. Bone weary, he knew that he would need to resume his quest tomorrow, so he turned in for the night.

That night, he dreamed again, as he had suspected he might. This time, Angela was younger, and she was dancing to the lively fiddle music at one of the numerous parties that she had loved to attend. Her partner was a younger girl whom he recognized as Cassandra Grey, one of the family members who had perished in a fire years ago in that terrible accident for which Angela now blamed him.

He noticed that his granddaughter was more excited to dance with Cassandra than she had been with any of the young male suitors who had unsuccessfully courted her in her youth. When the music stopped, Angela bent to speak in Cassandra's ear, and they both laughed, eyes alive with the sparkle of youth. Then his gaze was drawn to Cassandra's shadow, flickering in the firelight, and he saw that it was growing larger and blacker. He wanted to cry out to warn them both, but they were oblivious to the danger. Cassandra finally turned to see that her shadow was climbing her body, which began to shrivel and decompose. She tried to scream, but before she could do so, she disintegrated, leaving Angela confused and alone, uncertain of what had happened.

He woke with a start before dawn. George clambered out of the master berth and switched on the cabin light. He wanted to explore the meaning of the dream while it was still fresh in his mind, so he retrieved his tarot cards and necklace from his trunk and went back into the dining salon to sit at the table. "Guardian, friend, attend me now," he intoned, as he had done the day before. Almost immediately he felt the chill of the spirit's presence. But before he could begin to lay out the cards, the lights went out. He knew that the boat was connected to dock power, so there was no ordinary reason for all light to be lost, particularly since his boat's batteries would have taken over in the event of an outage. He waited calmly for this omen to manifest itself.

He wasn't disappointed. At first, the tapping was no louder than the other random sounds of a boat moored at a marina. But it grew louder, drowning out the slapping of water and the faint ringing of lines hanging from the boat spars. The tapping was rhythmic and moved around, first coming from the front, then from his right, then behind, and finally from his left. It was slowly circling him, and he caught himself following its movement with his eyes. The darkness was absolute, but when his eyes adjusted, he saw a reddish, glowing shape outlined in the air. As soon as he noticed it, it grew in size and he had to concentrate to keep from flinching. His Guardian would protect him from danger, and if it could not, nothing he could do would prevent a more powerful foe from harming him.

The shape settled in front of him, like a human guest sitting at the table. Then, in the faintest of voices, it began to taunt him. "Georgie, Georgie, Georgie."

He said nothing, only inclining his head to indicate his willingness to listen.

"So strong, so strong is Georgie." It made a hissing sound

that could have been a kind of laughter. "But Georgie is not strong enough. He is old. He is failing."

"It is true; I may not be strong enough," he rumbled. "Let us test my strength."

"Oh no!" It recoiled slightly. "I come not to test my Georgie, my pet."

He saw a face then, one of infinite beauty, long and angular. He shivered with a sudden chill and coughed. Glaring at the visage of the spirit, he raised a fist in the air. "Then begone, and send another who will speak truth and not meaningless riddles," he shouted.

The spirit did not fade. It hissed again. "Georgie is proud, too."

George lowered his hand and placed it carefully in front of him. "I am not proud. I am afraid for Angela."

The form shifted uncomfortably. "Speak not that name, for it is she who is to fall."

George knew he must press this spectral being for answers. Once such a creature volunteered definite information, he knew it would be willing to negotiate for more. "What is the bargain, spirit? What is the price for your knowledge?" he asked, once more courteous.

The spirit moved again, drifting to the right until it was positioned at the companionway leading to the master cabin. "An offering of light," it whispered.

George rose and walked toward the form, which dissolved into darkness as he approached. He was careful not to try turning on any electric lights, as artificial illumination would banish the presence. He felt his way back to the cabin and went to the large chest at the foot of the berth. Opening it, he fumbled amongst the boxes and bags until he felt warmth under his fingers. As he lifted out the cloth-wrapped item, his chest cramped with sadness. It was a ring, a memento of his wife, dead for many years. She had been, he had said, his light in the world. As he looked at the ring, he understood the bitter irony of the spirit's request. The spirit would take the essence of this item, and it would be up to George to destroy the ring's physical form, no matter how much that might hurt him.

He closed the trunk and returned to the dining salon. Sitting down, he unwrapped the ring and placed it on the table and waited. A moment later, the form coalesced in the darkness, still no more than a reddish afterglow such as George might see if he closed his eyes, but hissing with pleasure. The shape hovered over the ring, and George felt a cool breeze on his skin and a sinking feeling in the pit of his stomach. The spirit had taken what it wanted, leaving a physical ring emptied of meaning.

"For this light, I give you two warnings and one more warning. Beware the Soul Thief, the son of Beng, who stalks your family now."

George's ears rang with the shock of it. A demon, stalking his family? He almost didn't hear the next warning.

"Go not to the place of healing, for it shall be your doom."

Place of healing? This must refer to the hospital where Angela worked. He mulled that over, but he knew he could promise nothing that interfered with saving Angela.

The spirit mocked him again. "Georgie, Georgie, Georgie. Seek not the past, for if you do, your angel shall surely fall."

There was a long-drawn-out hiss, and the form melted away.

George sat motionless for a moment and then sprang to his feet. "Begone, spirits of night!" The light came on suddenly, and the electric warmth banished all shadows, revealing an ordinary dining salon. He went back to the master cabin and recorded his vision in his journal, wishing— not for the first time—that he could still work with his peers and compare his impressions with theirs. He knew that even with an active Guardian, a chovihano could fall prey to delusion when working alone. He had not worked with spirits since the accident, so he was especially vulnerable to their deceptions.

After writing, he heated a pot of water and brewed chamomile tea. He was tempted to remain awake but knew he would need all of his strength in the coming days. While waiting for the water to boil, he went to the head and washed his face and hands thoroughly, cleansing himself of the stink of the spirit world. The whistling kettle helped to further bring him back to earth, and he poured the water over the dried tea in a cracked cup. The tea's familiar flavor calmed him enough that by the time he had finished drinking a cup, drowsiness was stealing over him. Returning to the master cabin, he got back in bed and slept peacefully the rest of the night.

The café was crowded for breakfast when George arrived. He informed the greeter that he was looking for a friend and walked into the café to search for Eric. Just as George saw him waiting at a window table, the young man rose from his seat. George walked over to greet him.

"George, I'm glad we could talk," Eric said.

"I am also," said George, and they sat. A waitress brought menus, but George was unable to force himself to read his, so he set it down. Eric had already ordered coffee, but George could not stomach it yet. "I am worried about Angela."

Eric put down his menu, too, and sighed. "We both are." He steepled his fingers and closed his eyes, pausing for a moment as George anxiously watched him. Then he opened his eyes again and looked pensively at George. "I know that you and she aren't talking."

George nodded sadly. "Yes. We have been almost strangers for years now."

Eric placed his hands flat on the table, palms down. "She needs you now. Is there anything you can do to reconcile with her?"

George shook his head. "I do not have a problem with my Angela. She is very angry with me, though. About five years ago, there was a terrible accident. I cannot tell you what happened. It is a private matter. But she blames me for what happened, and I cannot make her see that I did not cause it."

"I know she worries about you."

George looked at Eric, surprised. "She does? She has sent me away every time we have spoken."

"Yeah, I remember she said something had come between you. I know that she is feeling overwhelmed at work and is going through a rough time."

George thumped the table. "I know!" Several other patrons looked around at them, and George lowered his voice. "I know. I want to help her."

Eric drummed his fingers. "Okay. Tell you what I'll do: I'll ask her to go out with me to a show. We were planning on doing something fun anyway, and maybe I can get her to reach out to you."

"You will do that? You are a good friend," George said. "I am sorry that I have not been very nice to you."

Eric grinned. "It's okay, George. Just because it's the twenty-first century, it doesn't mean everyone's on board with who I am. So long as we both love Angela, that's what matters."

George smiled with relief. "Very good. Okay, I am very hungry." He picked up the menu.

They gave the waitress their orders and spent the remainder of the morning engaged in small talk. When the meal was over, Eric paid the tab, and the two men shook hands.

"Call me when you have spoken with Angela, okay?"

"I'll do that," Eric replied.

They parted ways, and George drove back to the marina. Difficult as it was, he knew he would have to wait for Angela to call him. The last thing he wanted to do was to further alienate her.

I HATE You My Love

You were a shadow
Stretching far behind me
Mocking me
And I hated you
And then I saw you
A beautiful radiant angel
And I adored you
But you could not see me
Or hear me
And I hated you
And I showed you
Death
And you cried
And I adored you
But you left me
To be with him
And I hated you
And I adored you
- C

5.

THE NEXT day, Angela decided to dream-walk with Cassandra. Her patient was sedated, and Angela knew that the walk would help her navigate the girl's unconscious without the drama that frequently accompanied waking patients, though there would also be fewer clues regarding her troubled mind. The limited knowledge she would obtain would, nevertheless, give her a starting point in understanding Cassandra and, if possible, the apparent psychic talent she possessed.

Angela entered Cassandra's treatment room and saw that Cassandra was indeed asleep. The attending nurse was just leaving the room.

"I'll only be a moment, Joan. Thank you."

The nurse nodded and left. Angela went to the door, locked it, and sat in a chair near Cassandra's head. She stared at her sleeping face for a moment, remembering the child who had danced so happily years before and then had, so she thought, perished in agony in the fire that took the lives of her family. Angela sighed. "I hope I don't regret this."

She reached out and touched Cassandra's forehead. Cassandra twitched and moaned but did not awaken. Angela felt the familiar dropping sensation in the pit of her stomach. Cassandra's face blurred and shifted for a moment.

Angela muttered, "Talk to me. Talk..." Without fanfare, she found herself standing in the otherworldly meadow under a night sky. The scene was dreamlike, as if seen underwater. She knew that this was a side effect of the sedation.

Angela said again, "Talk to me." There was no answer, but she had not really expected any. She was alone in the dark meadow. Angela turned slowly, looking all around. Her heartbeat quickened, and sweat cooled on her forehead. Expecting to see the vast shadow or hear the voices, she called out in what she hoped was a confident tone. "I know you're here. I saw you when I was with Roger."

She spread her hands in a peaceful gesture. "I mean you no harm." She suspected that the shadow had been the trauma lurking in Cassandra's unconscious, and she hoped that this initial walk might cause it to show in some form. But there was no evidence of anything untoward.

"I'm going to admit you," Angela said. "We'll work through this. I will be your..." She swallowed, her mouth dry. "Chovihani."

There was a flicker in the air. A scene materialized not far from where Angela was standing. A small half-Rom girl that Angela recognized as the child Cassandra was running on a dusty road, playing and laughing. She stopped and looked toward Angela. The road faded, leaving young Cassandra and Angela facing each other.

"Who're you?" said the girl.

Angela squatted down to talk. "Hi. I'm Angela. What's your name?"

"Cassie. Are you a witch?"

Angela rocked back on her heels, startled. "Well... maybe I am, and maybe I'm not. What do you think?"

Cassandra said, "You look like a witch. Can you tell my fortune?" She held out a very dirty hand. Before Angela could react, the girl turned her head, as if hearing a voice. She glanced back at Angela. "I gotta go. Mama's calling." Cassandra turned and started to run.

"Wait! Cassie, will you come back here again?"

Cassandra yelled over her shoulder. "Yeah!"

Cassandra disappeared. Angela stood slowly, exhausted already. Staring at the ground, she walked over to a patch of floor tile, took a step, and the walls of the hospital room reappeared. Angela was still sitting by Cassandra's side, but she was breathing heavily and felt very sweaty. Angela brushed Cassandra's forehead tenderly then removed her hand. Cassandra remained deeply asleep. Angela rose slowly to her feet, unlocked the door, and left the room. This wasn't going to be easy, she knew, but having made some contact with the pre-trauma self within Cassandra was very encouraging.

Angela decided that the best thing for her to do was to take care of mundane matters in her office until the shift was over. Tomorrow, she would begin prepping the other patients in her study and start their legitimate treatments with the rTMS. Knowing that Cassandra would require her more unusual talents, she would need to be careful how much time she gave the teenager in order to avoid arousing suspicion.

Angela awoke with a start, her heart thudding in her chest. She glanced at the clock and swore. Three o'clock in the morning. She had spent the remainder of the day thinking about her work with Cassandra, and when she had finally gone home, she had lain awake in bed, unable to sleep until after midnight. Of course, she had dreamed, and a particularly disturbing nightmare had awakened her.

After a few more minutes staring into the darkened room, she got out of bed, switched on the light, and went into her home office. Sitting down at her desk, she opened her laptop and found her electronic journal. For a moment, she waited for inspiration to help her describe what she saw, but then she gave up and started typing.

"Tonight I dreamed that I had two lovers. One was the man whom I have seen in other dreams, and the other was a woman. We were all sharing a bed together, making love, and then somehow I realized that the man was trying to kill the woman and have me for himself. I threw them both out of bed and we started arguing. That's when it got weird. Every time I tried to say something, the other two would say the same thing, so that we were speaking in unison. But when one of them spoke, everything was normal. Then it was as if the woman and I merged into one being, and the man became afraid and ran away. My psychiatrist colleagues would have a field day with this one."

She snapped the lid shut and sat in silence for a few more minutes. Ordinarily, she would dismiss the dream as an expression of anxiety or frustrated libido, but her intuition, which she usually trusted, said it was otherwise. She needed to find the root of the dream within herself. When she used dream-walking for healing, she would explore the patient's deep mind, represented by the forest surrounding the "meadow" of the conscious self. Usually an omen would manifest itself in the form of a person or animal that would perform a significant action or bring a message, which would help to illuminate the patient's complaint

Taking a deep, calming breath, she decided that it was time to dream-walk for herself. She had not done this for years, so she felt uncertain. Angela returned to her bedroom and dressed hurriedly, choosing sensible hiking clothes, as she had no idea where she would end up on the other side of this excursion. Secreting her ID in a money belt, she stood in the center of the room, took a deep breath, and closed her eyes. With her right hand, she touched her forehead then her sternum, and murmured the key words her grandfather had taught her to help unlock her talent when using it that way.

She felt the familiar dropping sensation in the pit of her stomach, and a sudden breeze caressed her cheeks. When she opened her eyes, she squinted against the glare of bright sunlight and saw that she was standing in a clearing in the woods. She turned in place, orienting herself in what was, for her, a familiar place. To one side of the clearing was a lean-to, somewhat weatherworn but in good condition. She walked over to it, opened the door, and retrieved a walking staff. Squaring her shoulders, she hiked to the edge of the woods and found a path.

At first, the woods were open and pleasant, and she thanked herself for the years of work she had undertaken to dredge up repressed emotions and unpleasant memories. But soon, as she walked the winding path, the trees grew closer together, and when she crossed a small brook, she sensed a transition. She slowed her steps and began watching in all directions, her spine tingling. Here was the zone of the deeper unconscious, where she expected to find the trigger for tonight's odd dream.

Between one step and the next, she stumbled as the ground shifted beneath her feet. She used her staff to prevent a fall and looked around. She was soon standing in a garden under an evening sky. Her breath caught in her throat at the beauty of it, and she shivered with a sense of recognition. The garden was arranged in the English style, with formal straight and curved paths that converged on a gazebo in front of her. She cautiously drew near the structure and stopped when she saw several people in it. At that moment, they looked at her and waved, so she resumed her approach. She realized that she no longer had her walking staff, and glancing down, she saw that she was dressed in multicolored robes. She was unsurprised to see that her hands had six fingers.

She looked back up and saw that those awaiting her were a man and a woman. They were the lovers of her dream, but they were taller, and as she approached, she felt a growing sense of familiarity. The man was the one from other dreams, but the woman strongly resembled Cassandra. They smiled, and the woman stretched her open arms in a gesture of welcome. Angela approached them. The man stood to one side, smiling, but not quite as openly as the woman. When Angela embraced the woman, a shock of grief ran through her, as if she were embracing the memory of a long-dead friend.

No one had spoken, and later Angela would wonder about that. But in the garden, silence seemed natural. Angela stepped back and looked at the man, expecting another warm welcome. But his back was turned, and she felt his cold disapproval with dismay. She wanted to comfort him and reassure him, but something prevented her from touching him.

The woman grasped Angela's hand and looked searchingly into her eyes. Then, with a sinking feeling, Angela realized that this was, indeed, a version of Cassandra. As that realization struck home, her surroundings rippled. Looking down at her feet, she saw that she was standing on a tiled piece of flooring rather than the stone flags of the gazebo. Her ears popped as the gazebo and garden were swept away and replaced with an unexpected sight.

She was standing in the darkened hospital room where they had put Cassandra.

She hadn't moved like that in a very long time, not since her grandfather had taught her to control her dream-walks. She usually strayed no farther than a few feet from where she started and almost never moved physically when dream-walking for another person. Angela had never found a satisfactory explanation for the phenomenon, and ascribed it to sleepwalking, even though she had at times found herself in locked rooms or impossible circumstances. Tiptoeing to avoid waking Cassandra, she opened the door and left the room.

"Dr. Cooper?"

Turning, Angela saw the night-duty nurse at her station. "Joan. I was... checking on Cassandra. Patient C."

Joan was frowning in puzzlement. "I didn't see you come in, Doctor. I don't think I fell asleep."

Angela laughed nervously. "I have my ways. No, you weren't asleep. I wouldn't worry about it. I'm heading back home now, so have a nice night." She was talking too rapidly.

"Very well," Joan replied, though Angela could almost read her thoughts. Angela had developed a reputation amongst hospital staff as a maverick, known for her unorthodox methods and for keeping odd hours, so this would be one more strange event to be discussed and, she hoped, forgotten.

Angela left the hospital, caught a taxi, and returned home to pass the short remainder of the morning in dreamless sleep.

Later that morning, Angela began her day by collating the case histories of her trial patients on the newly repaired iMac. Fortunately, she had made good progress the previous afternoon, so the work was going quickly. She was nursing her third cup of coffee and staring abstractedly at the portrait of Carl Jung on the wall when the desk phone rang, and she picked it up. "Dr. Cooper."

"Hey, Angela." It was Eric.

"Oh, hey." Belatedly she realized that she had promised to go out that night, and she kicked herself mentally for not canceling.

"Are you busy tonight? There's that gorgeous show at the Cabaret. You've got to come."

Angela said, "I—You know, I'm really busy now. We've started prepping patients for the clinical trial, and I need to put all my energy into that work."

"That's great news! Let's celebrate!"

"I'm really sorry. I just don't have time." She knew this wasn't what he wanted to hear.

"Hon, didn't we talk about this? You work too hard."

Angela sighed. "I know. It's just, there's a new patient, and she's going to need my personal attention."

"Oh, Angela. You've got to take care of yourself or you'll

burn out."

Angela started straightening the papers on her desk, phone pressed to her ear. "This is really important to me, Eric. Try to understand, okay?"

He sighed. "You're blowing me off, aren't you? It's okay; Eric still loves you. Listen, when you come up for air, give me a call, okay? Soon?"

"Okay. Thanks for understanding. I really appreciate it."

"Just don't forget to call. Bye." He hung up.

She knew that he was right and that she should pace herself. But Cassandra's problem was too urgent, and she felt that there wasn't much time to solve the puzzle. When she got those hunches they were usually correct. That afternoon, she planned to begin treating Cassandra, and it would require all of her concentration to do so.

Angela went to Cassandra's treatment room, accompanied by an orderly. She found Cassandra sitting up in bed, unmoving, staring at Angela.

Angela smiled. "Hi, Cassandra. How are you feeling today?"

Cassandra was mute. Angela took a seat by her bed.

"Today we're going to just talk. I want to get to know you better so I can help you." Angela nodded at the orderly, who left the room. She then got up and locked the door, and turning back to Cassandra, she felt a familiar calm wash over her. She was ready to begin. "Okay, Cassie. If I'm going to be your chovihani, you have to respect me and my work."

Cassandra watched Angela silently and then nodded. Her eyes moved to stare past Angela at the window. Angela resisted the urge to look at the window as well.

"Now, please lie down, Cassie. I need to touch your forehead, and you might pass out when I do."

Cassandra continued to stare, unmoving. A chill washed down Angela's spine.

"Cassandra? Can you hear me?"

"Are you looking for me? I can see you, but you can't see me."

Angela said, "Cassandra? What do you mean, I can't see you?" Her heart beat faster. It was happening again.

"You're weak. I will come to you, and then I will take your gift," said Cassandra in a flat voice.

Angela knew it was time to take the battle to the enemy. "All right then. Let's do this."

She reached out and touched Cassandra on the forehead. Two things happened simultaneously. Cassandra jerked backward, awkward in her seated position, her face registering shock, and the room filled with voices.

"No-o-o! Don't touch me!" Cassandra shouted.

Angela stood. The light grew dim as if a shadow had passed over the window. She saw, superimposed over the walls, the ghostly image of the trees surrounding the meadow in the Otherworld, as the room faded. Angela scanned the meadow and kept a hand outstretched in Cassandra's direction. "Cassandra, I'm here. We are almost in the Otherworld now."

Cassandra was panting. "What are you talking about?" She clearly did not see what Angela could see. She looked at Angela, and a puzzled frown creased her forehead.

"Mama? Is that you?"

"No, Cassandra, I'm Dr. Cooper. You're safe here."

Cassandra's voice trembled. "You'll die. It's going to eat you like it's eating me."

The trees had grown vividly detailed and made a rustling sound. There was a distinct shadow visible on the horizon. Angela dropped her clipboard and reached out to Cassandra. The teenager pulled away, but Angela was quicker. She grabbed Cassandra's shoulder and stared into her face. "Cassandra. Look at me."

Cassandra's eyes darted as she panicked, and the whispering voices grew louder. Then Angela almost let go, startled, as Cassandra's face seemed to shatter into pieces. Faces of women and men appeared within a kaleidoscope of color, and bright light flared in Angela's peripheral vision. This was unexpected, but Angela had seen stranger things in her many forays into the Otherworld.

"Cassandra, you are awake. You are here. You can hear my voice. Listen to me."

Cassandra's gaze settled on Angela. Her eyes widened and her mouth opened to scream. Angela reached out with her other hand and grasped Cassandra's shoulders. The women stood close to each other, and Cassandra twisted in Angela's grasp.

"It's okay," Angela said. "You're okay. Shhh. You're safe. You're in a safe place. Look at me."

Cassandra's eyes welled with tears. "I gotta get... out..."

Suddenly, the forest vanished, along with the shadow. Cassandra collapsed, almost dragging Angela to the floor, but Angela was able to lower her gently and kneel by her side.

Both were sweating, and the room was crackling with the energy of what had just happened.

Cassandra began weeping softly. "Mama..."

Angela hugged her and rocked her. "I'm here to help, Cassie. Can I call you Cassie? We'll do this together, okay?"

"Okay." Cassandra's voice was muffled as she pressed her face to Angela's chest. Angela squeezed her shoulders and paused for a moment. Cassandra shifted her face, nuzzling, and her hands squeezed a little tighter. Uncomfortable, Angela released Cassandra and got to her feet.

"I need to go now. Are you going to be okay?"

Cassandra nodded. Angela knew that she would recall the experience as if it had been a dream, forgetting the details but benefiting, she hoped, from the therapy. "I'll be back tomorrow morning, and we can do some more. We'll get through this, Cassandra."

Angela helped Cassandra back to the bed and turned to leave. Closing the door, she walked over to the duty nurse's station across from the room entrance. "Ginny, please continue with the micro-dosages of antipsychotics and monitor this patient. If she stabilizes, we'll start the trial tomorrow."

Ginny looked up at Angela. "Yes." For a moment, Angela thought her voice echoed oddly. She looked more closely at the nurse then shook her head and left. She was tired, but she felt growing excitement. She knew she should be more enthusiastic about the trial, which was scheduled to start right away, but she was completely distracted by the work she was doing with Cassandra. Though it was Friday, she knew that her best option was to work through the weekend to maintain the momentum in treating the troubled teenager. In order to avoid the appearance of impropriety, she would also begin the trial with her next patient, a man named Daniel, tomorrow.

That evening, Angela arrived home very late and collapsed onto the couch. She stared out at the Bay Area skyline, too tired to move and too numb to think. She knew that the daily dream-walks were taking a toll, but the urgent need to help Cassandra drove her mercilessly. Not for the first time, she wished she had been drawn to a different calling, one that was not so exhausting and that did not tempt her to use that extraordinary talent.

Soon she drifted into a half-awake state of reverie, remembering the times when she freely used her talent for the benefit of others. She could not recall ever feeling this drained, though, and she wondered if something else was sapping her energy. She unwound memories back to her adolescence, seeking clues to her current problems.

Angela had had her first dream-walk at the age of twelve, when she awakened one night in her pajamas several blocks from home in downtown Ballard. She had been dreaming that she was in a clearing at night and had felt a sense of freedom and happiness that made her run and skip for joy, the starlit grass whipping around her feet. She approached the verge of the forest, which appeared to be open and friendly, park-like and clear. She found a path and continued skipping, singing to herself, when she saw flickering light ahead. She stopped running, cautious even in her sleep, and approached a campfire. Sitting next to it was a hunched figure, humming and tending a small pot to one side of the fire.

"Hello?" Angela stood in the shadows at the edge of the campsite.

The figure stopped humming, raised its hands, and lowered a cowl. Angela felt a thrill of fear and backed away as the figure turned. Then she ran in panic. She crashed into trees, tripped over underbrush that had not been there just moments before, and careened blindly along the path until her feet struck a hard, solid surface. The unexpected, jolting change in texture made her fall to her knees, skinning one of them. She kneeled, sobbing, until the quality of the air changed and the fog of sleep lifted from her mind. When she looked up, she was kneeling on pavement, and she stood to find herself far from home and wide awake. The ever-present drizzle was rapidly dampening her pajamas and plastering them to her thin frame. She stood, shivering, in the middle of the wet street until oncoming headlights skidded and narrowly avoided her. The blaring horn as the car's taillights receded awoke her from her trance, and she stumbled, sobbing helplessly, to the sidewalk.

The police found her that night and, after questioning her gently, called her grandfather. George, who had raised her since childhood after her parents died in an auto accident, took her home, warmed her with hot soup, and reassured her that she would be all right. Though cold and exhausted, she was terrified of falling asleep and dreaming again. George promised her that he would catch the dreams and make them leave her alone, and after much coaxing, he persuaded her to return to bed. After she drifted off to sleep, he conferred with his sister, the Rom seeress Nadia, who told him that she had had a vision of Angela running in the night.

Angela and her grandfather had later moved to San Francisco. His boatbuilding business had been slowing in the Puget Sound area, due to the economic downturn, and he had heard that there were a lot of wealthy clients in the Bay Area who would gladly hire him for his woodworking skills. He was becoming famous on the West Coast for his beautifully handcrafted boats, which he finished with the colorful details of the Roma caravans.

George had come to believe that public school was inadequate to help train his granddaughter's brilliant mind, so he had taken that task upon himself, homeschooling her until she enrolled at Berkeley at the age of sixteen. He had taught himself everything that he needed to know, or so he thought, but she had proven to be a special challenge, questioning his authority and complaining that she felt caged by his enforced discipline.

When Angela was fourteen, she had had another dreamwalking experience. One night, as she slept in her cabin in the large sailboat that they lived aboard, she dreamed that she was flying freely, escaping the confines of her life. The moonlit sky was unusually vivid, and below her was a carpet of trees, dotted with clearings. Ahead, she saw a cliff and a vast sea beyond it, and on a whim, she swooped down. The cliff knoll dropped hundreds of feet to the ocean on one side, and to the other, several hundred feet away, the forest brooded.

She landed, and in the moment of landing, she staggered with heaviness. Whereas in flight she had felt light and bodiless, on the ground, she was dressed in her pajamas and had human form, and she had to shield her eyes from brilliance as night became day. She looked around at the grass-covered knoll that rose gently to the cliff, and at the deep-blue sky above, dotted with clouds, and took great lungfuls of air. She laughed and twirled in place, dancing with delight in her freedom.

A movement caught her attention, and she looked at the woods. She gasped when she saw animals gathering at the edge. There were deer, raccoons, bears, and squirrels, and they began moving slowly toward her while birds flew in her direction. She felt a wave of love for them and walked toward them as they approached. Soon, she was surrounded by them, petting deer and stroking the fur of the bears while squirrels and birds perched on her shoulders.

As she acquainted herself with the woodland creatures, she saw a movement out of the corner of her eye and turned to look. Someone, whether male or female she could not tell, was striding confidently out of the forest. The person was dressed from head to toe in green that rustled, and as this person neared, Angela realized that he—she?—was covered in leaves that were artfully woven into a garment.

The animals parted to create a clear path. Angela looked into bright, curious eyes, and felt an unexpected surge of desire. She had awakened to her sexuality recently, and now she felt herself becoming warm. Unselfconsciously, she opened her arms and embraced the stranger. There, on the grass, she and the person in green made love. She determined that her partner was a boy. She had never experienced this kind of intimacy, and it was breathtaking. As she explored her partner's body, though, she was startled to discover female sexual organs as well. This was unexpected, but not entirely unwelcome, as Angela had felt curiosity about both genders.

It seemed as if she were there for hours, engaged in passionate love play, when a chill breeze sprang up. Her partner leaped up, smiled fleetingly, and dashed off, deaf to Angela's cries to stay. Angela got up slowly, still surrounded by the animals, and saw that the light was growing dim. There was a new odor of cut grass that came out of nowhere, and when she looked down, she realized she was standing on a mowed patch amidst the wildflowers and tall grasses of the knoll. Then, without any warning, the world around her faded away.

She found herself in the front yard of a stranger's home in the predawn dark, shivering in her pajamas and squinting in the glare of security spotlights. It took a lot of fast-talking, and a few tears, to convince the homeowner that she was not intentionally trespassing but had sleepwalked. Hours later, after her grandfather had fetched her home, she was still unable to explain to herself what had happened.

The next day, George questioned her regarding her sleepwalking. "Angel, how could you have walked so far?"

He was not angry, she was relieved to see, but worried. Angela struggled with her own uncertainty and then decided to come clean. She told him everything she had experienced, though she omitted the lovemaking with the animal boy, and watched George's eyes widen in surprise. At one point during her description, George sprang to his feet in the narrow dining salon, clutching his hair. When Angela had finished, he stood by one of the portholes and gazed out.

"This is incredible news," he said finally. "You have a gift denied to most, even among those of us with the Sight." He turned back to her. "Angel, you must learn how to control your walking in the dream world—your dream-walking. It is a great power that you have, and if you do not seek to control it, it will dominate you and it could destroy you." His serious tone frightened her. She had never seen her grandfather so agitated before.

"Granddad, I didn't mean to... to dream-walk," she said. "It just happened. How can I control it?"

He came over and sat next to her, clasping her hands in his own large, work-hardened fingers. "Just like you control everything else. With discipline, and learning, and understanding." He got up and went to the master cabin. She heard him rummaging in the big chest that she was never allowed to open, and he came back with a small pouch and a fabric-wrapped box. He opened the box, and she suppressed a grin of excitement. He was going to read the cards!

"Okay. You know what to do," he said, handing her the cards. While she shuffled and cut the deck, he lit a small candle and laid a silk cloth on the dining table. When she was done shuffling, she handed the deck back to him and he began turning over cards in a classic cross pattern, the snap of cards sounding like the ticking of a clock.

Her grandfather frowned at the reading, and she leaned over for a better view. She saw a juggling man, another man who looked like a priest, but he was upside down, and a card showing a large bundle of sticks on a man's back. She glanced up at her grandfather, who was muttering to himself.

"So that's the way of it." He looked back at Angela, and his features softened. "My Angel, it seems that I must train you."

She started to speak but stopped when she saw him frown. "This is not our way," he continued. "The chovihano trains the man, the chovihani trains the woman. But your great-aunt Nadia is not taking any more students. This card here," and he indicated the priest, "says that it is I who must train you. This one," pointing to the man carrying the sticks, "says that it will be very hard work. And here..." He picked up the juggling man and held it up for Angela to see. "This one says that you will become a great magician but that you must deceive others to do your work."

He swept up the cards, re-cased them, and snuffed the candle. George leaned toward Angela, his face serious. "What did you think about before going to sleep last night?"

"I don't remember."

George reached across the table and gently tapped her forehead. Angela saw a brief burst of light, and her mind cleared. "I was thinking about how much fun we had sailing, and about our neighbor and how goofy he looked in his sailor clothes, and... about the handsome boy who was visiting at the next dock." Here she blushed, but George didn't appear to notice. "Then, I thought about Mom and Dad and how much I wished I could see them again."

This time, George's face creased in worry lines, and he lifted his hand again and stroked her hair. "Not a day goes by that I do not think of them, my Angel. Their spirits have left our world on a journey in the Otherworld." Then he paused, and a startled look came over his face. "That is it! The Otherworld."

He got up again and went back to the master cabin.

"Granddad? What're you talking about?"

His voice came back to her. "That is where you went. Somehow you are able to walk in body to the Otherworld."

Angela's heart caught in her throat, and her mouth was dry. "Does that mean I... died?"

George emerged from the cabin. "No! You can go there while you are alive. Do you see? You can go to where people like me can only see with difficulty after long training." He was carrying a larger bag that jingled, and he set it down on the table and began removing his shirt. Angela watched as her grandfather donned a different, brightly embroidered shirt and a handful of necklaces. He pinned metal badges to the shirt. Lastly, he wrapped his head with a red scarf then sat back down.

Angela was fighting the urge to laugh. He looked ridiculous in those clothes, like a bearded peacock, but when she saw his glittering eyes, the urge to laugh vanished. A palpable sense of power emanated from him, and she felt a momentary chill. Then he smiled, and the warmth of his smile reassured her.

"Angel, I will be your chovihano. We are going to learn how you walk in the Otherworld, and how to make it happen when you want it to, and how to stop when you want to stop." He reached across the table and clasped her hands. "Today we will have our first lesson. Look at my eyes. No, do not look out the window. Look at my eyes and relax."

Angela looked in his eyes and felt as if she were both sinking down and rising up. A detached lassitude overcame her, and she waited, passively, for him to tell her what to do next.

"Good. You are a very apt student. Now, my voice is all you can hear. I will count backward from ten, and when I have reached zero, you will be asleep. Ten... nine..."

George led Angela through a standard induction into hypnotic trance and questioned her regarding her dream-walking experience. Even entranced, she was reluctant to tell him about her sexual encounter, but she told him everything else, including things that she had consciously forgotten. He became excited when she told him about the patch of mown grass, and he speculated that she returned by finding a place that existed in both worlds at that moment.

Over the next few days, George was able to discover a few more salient points concerning Angela's talent but could not find a way for her to prevent unwanted sleepwalks. Her excursions increased in frequency, and though most of them did not result in physical movement, all of the dream-walks left evidence that Angela had been bodily present in the Otherworld. One night she came back with muddy feet, and another night she returned to find herself standing in the kitchenette with a bloody knee, scraped from a hard fall that she had taken while running.

The first breakthrough came, interestingly enough, when she experienced a daytime dream-walk. It happened while she was jogging before lunch. She rounded a corner and collided with another jogger, a slightly older woman. They accidentally embraced, and Angela's hand brushed the other woman's forehead as she extricated herself. She felt a whirling sensation, and her stomach sank, and the world shifted around her. She found herself standing in the forest meadow like where she always started, but this time she was not alone. The jogger was with her there, and they both stood on an incongruous patch of concrete in the middle of the meadow. They stared at each other for a moment, and then the jogger opened her mouth to scream. Then, without warning, the dream-walk ended, leaving them back where they started.

"God, what the hell—" said the woman, who then doubled over and retched on the sidewalk. Angela backed away, her heart thudding, and then she ran blindly. When she realized that she was about to dash into traffic, she found a bench and sat, panting heavily. A passerby stopped and asked if she was okay, and she replied that yes, she was fine, and that she was just winded. Angela could not think clearly. Her mind was racing, and she could not stop thinking about how out of control her talent was becoming. Finally, she calmed enough to begin walking back to the boat.

When she got there, she found George cleaning the deck.

"Granddad, I dream-walked," she said without preamble. He dropped his swabbing brush in shock and stared at her for a moment.

"Are you okay, Angel?" He hurried over. He looked carefully at her then sniffed the air. "There is that smell again. You were in the Otherworld." He had never explained what he smelled, but he had told her he could always tell when she had been there.

"Can we go inside? I'm feeling tired," Angela said. It was true. She could not stop yawning, and on stumbling feet she went below, George following. She went to the settee in the dining cabin and sat heavily; then she leaned forward and rested her head in her arms. Within moments, she was snoring. George got a pillow to place under her head then waited anxiously by her side.

"Angel, what are we going to do?" he muttered.

After half an hour, she awoke to the sound of a whistling teakettle. George brought over two cups. "Here, drink this. It will make you feel better." They both sipped the tea. Then Angela set her tea down and looked at George.

"I was just jogging, and I ran into a woman coming the other way. Then, bam, we were there. It just lasted a moment, and we were back, but she really freaked out."

George looked thoughtful. "Could it be that you can touch another person to dream-walk? But then we hug, and you have many friends that you touch and dance with. And you dream-walk by yourself. It must be something else that you were doing. May I hypnotize you again?"

Angela's reply was immediate. "Yes. Right now."

George left to change, and when he came back in what he called his sorcerer's clothes, Angela was already lying on the settee. He hypnotized her and questioned her about what had happened. As the details emerged, one thing stood out: her act of brushing the forehead of the woman.

When she emerged from trance an hour later, George told her what he was thinking.

"So maybe I need to touch someone's forehead. That sounds weird," she said.

"Maybe it is, as you say, weird. But we can try that right now. Touch my forehead."

Angela shrank back. "Granddad, please, not right now. That

scared the hell out of me." He frowned at her language. "Sorry, but it did."

George relented. "Okay, but that is something we should explore."

Later, after she had recovered further, they did try this, and the dream-walk caught them both up into the meadow. George's expression of wonder at finding himself in the Otherworld was almost comically intense, and Angela grew to take delight in her excursions, many of which were in his company. When Angela entered the Otherworld in George's company, she found herself in a forest meadow that differed substantially from her own. This one was very orderly, and there were several structures, including an ornately decorated cabin that they soon learned represented his shamanistic discipline and power.

As her training progressed, Angela learned how to create such structures for herself, including a small lean-to that would house the walking staff that she could use on her own journeys. Her grandfather attempted to teach her some of his other lore, but the only things she was able to learn were his invisibility trick—which distracted the mind of anyone observing her—and the use of her inner light. She actually surpassed him in her skill with invisibility, and this became a source of pride for him.

She learned about her inner light one afternoon during a training session. As they prepared to return to the physical world, Angela saw a strange illumination that seemed to come from her grandfather, though his body did not actually glow. When Angela asked him about it, he looked searchingly into her eyes. "This is the light of the soul. Your own light will shine when you are true to yourself and when you need to see into the dark places." He placed a hand on her shoulder. "This light will drive away all darkness, my Angel."

They took the steps that led back to the physical world, and as the shapes of the sailboat dining salon reappeared, George said, "Angel. Promise me something."

"Sure, Granddad."

"Promise me that you will not use your light to cause harm to any but only to defend the helpless."

She was puzzled. "What? You mean, like attack someone with lasers or something?"

"No," he replied solemnly. "I mean, do not use your light as if it were a weapon that could hurt."

"Why?"

"Because to do that, you would have to fill your heart with fear and hatred, and that would be your undoing."

Angela shrugged. "Sure, no problem. I've never met anyone that I wanted to hurt anyway."

One other thing that Angela and George learned was that only she could traverse physical distance while dream-walking. He always returned to physical awareness in the place where he started. Despite her experiences with such travel, Angela was never comfortable with the notion that she had physically entered the Otherworld, preferring instead to believe that it was a purely mental experience that occasionally resulted in a form of sleepwalking.

Over the ensuing years, Angela learned how to prevent involuntary dream-walks by using a series of gestures that would act as keys for her talent. She also learned how to find the evanescent clues that showed her how to return to the physical world. She was happy to note that she no longer felt tired after most dream-walking sessions, and she concluded that her regular practice strengthened whatever part of her gave her this power. However, the greatest use of her talent was revealed to her during her sixteenth birthday party at her great-aunt Nadia's house. One of her cousins had also been visiting and had been complaining of terrible nightmares.

"Nana," her cousin, a young girl named Florica, said, "can you give me a potion to help me sleep?"

Nadia made a clucking sound. "Flo, yes I can, but don't you think it's better if you learn what's causing your nightmares?"

The girl looked puzzled. "They're nightmares. Everybody has nightmares sometimes."

Nadia looked up at Angela who was standing nearby. "But I think that yours are special. Angela, maybe you can help your cousin here. I know that you've dream-walked with George."

Angela, surprised, replied, "But I've never seen anything that looked like a nightmare. I don't know what to do."

"I think you'll know when the time comes," Nadia said. "George has told me that you have a natural instinct for things of the Otherworld."

"I suppose so."

"Very well, then." Nadia got up and took Florica's hand. "Now, I want you to lie down on the couch here." She did so, and Nadia said, "Angela, I believe you know what to do."

Angela sat next to her cousin and touched her forehead. She immediately felt the sinking sensation that signaled a dream-walk. The physical world blurred, to be replaced with the familiar forest meadow. Her cousin was lying on the grass next to her, and when Florica's eyes opened, they opened even wider as she took a breath to scream. Angela covered her mouth. "Don't you dare scream. Can you see all this?" She gestured to the meadow around her. Her cousin nodded.

"I'm going to take my hand away. Can you be quiet?" She nodded again, so Angela removed her hand.

Florica sat up, trembling. "I... I can't believe it."

"You will." Angela looked more closely around her. It looked a bit like the meadow she saw when she dream-walked by herself, but there were differences. The trees were less forbidding and tall, and there were fewer brambles around the verge. She helped her cousin to stand, and they spent a moment taking in the scene. Florica clung to Angela until, irritated, Angela shook her off. "Let's look around."

The two girls began walking around the meadow, exploring the varied grasses and wildflowers and peering into the depths of the forest from the meadow's edge, though they did not attempt to go into it.

A sudden movement made Angela turn to face the trees. Coming out of the edge of the forest was a strange animal, shaped like a deer but with a fox's head. When Florica saw, it she yelped in panic. Angela caught her arm.

"Don't run away," she hissed. "I bet this is your nightmare." Angela pulled her cousin closer to her side. "Look it in the eyes and show it who's boss."

At first, Florica was reluctant to look at the beast and stood there shuddering and whimpering. Meanwhile, the creature crept closer. Angela noticed that the fox head was drooling.

"Gross. Florica, look, it's just gross. It's not scary at all."

"Eww," Florica said when she saw the thick streamers of saliva dangling from its jaws. Then she giggled. The creature stopped in its tracks. Both girls broke into laughter, causing the creature to whine piteously and lower its head and tail. Then, impulsively, Angela's cousin reached out her hand. The nightmare hesitantly approached and sighed when Florica touched its head. She scratched it between the ears, and its whine changed to a muted rumble, like the purring of a very large cat. After a few more moments of scratching both its head and neck, and exclaiming over the softness of its fur, Florica dropped her hand.

"Go home now," she said gently, smiling. The creature ducked its head, turned, and loped back into the forest. She and Angela looked at each other, and then Florica gave her cousin a hug. "Thank you, Angela. You are the greatest of the chovihani."

Angela blushed. "Flo, I'm not yet, but someday..." She paused, realizing that she was making a life decision. "Someday I will be a healer." She looked around at the clearing, and then she frowned.

"We've got to get back. Everyone's probably wondering where we went. Start looking for, I don't know, a patch of carpet or mowed grass or something."

They wandered in the vicinity of the center of the meadow, searching carefully. It was Florica who saw the patch of carpeting that looked very much like Great-Aunt Nadia's, so they both stood on it and watched it grow. Angela took one step, then another, and in a moment they were back in Nadia's trailer. The room was darkened and empty.

Angela called out, "Nana?"

She looked at her cousin, but Florica was pale, and subdued after their experience, she sat on the couch. Then Angela heard voices outside, and she opened the front door.

"There you are!" Nadia bustled back into the trailer. "I was looking all over for you two. When did you get back? You were gone for two hours!"

"Gone?"

Nadia settled back in her overstuffed chair. "Yes, gone. You disappeared."

"What did you see? Tell me what you saw when we went." Angela sat down on the couch next to her cousin.

"At first, you just sat there, fingers touching her forehead. Then you laid your head down on Florica's belly, and you both just drifted off to sleep." Nadia frowned. "Then I don't know how it happened. One minute, you were snoring, and I took my eyes off you for just a second. When I looked back, both of you were gone."

"That's what Granddad said, too. He's never seen me just disappear. It's always when he looks away, or blinks, or just drifts off. One time he tried to stare at me, and he said that it felt as if the world jumped, like he just slept for a second, and I was gone." Angela shivered. "I don't know. I'm learning about science, and science says that everything has an explanation. I just don't know what it is."

Nadia patted her hand. "Science doesn't know everything, Angel. One of these days you'll see that. When you do, come back to old Nana, and I'll tell you a thing or two that will raise your hair straight up." She chuckled. In the years after that episode, Angela had never found a reason to go back and ask her great-aunt what she had to tell her.

Angela remembered that Florica, having reclaimed her courage by confronting her "nightmare," cornered one of her brothers who had tormented her mercilessly as a younger child, demanded an apology, and got it.

Shaking herself out of her reverie, Angela got off the couch and stretched the kinks out of her back. Dream-walks had been very tiring before she had started her training all those years ago, she now remembered. Evidently, she was out of practice, but at least there was a reasonable explanation for her exhaustion.

That night her sleep was troubled by ordinary dreams that, thankfully, did not result in any spontaneous dream-walking. The next morning when she awoke, Angela was more determined than ever to assist Cassandra in her journey toward wholeness.

Cassandra lay back on her hospital bed and stared up at the ceiling, unable to sleep. The bed was comfortable enough, and for the moment the whispering she usually heard was almost silent. But her emotions were in turmoil. She could not stop thinking of Angela, how she had led Cassandra into that bizarre dream, and how she was full of light and power as she stood there, protecting Cassandra from the terrors of her own mind.

She had never been able to make a strong connection with any other person since the fire because of the voices. She had at times sought intimacy, but the few stolen moments with the occasional stranger had only accentuated her solitude. But now she felt a stirring of feelings for the first time in years.

A sibilant murmuring became evident again, and she resolutely ignored it.

—*Hold her down...*—

—*Why am I here?*—

—*Angela...*—

She sat up when she heard that. The voices sometimes spoke the names of people who were physically close to her, but she had not heard the name of Angela before. Rising up in her was, once again, a powerful protective impulse. She hugged herself in that dark room and, silently, swore that nothing would hurt her new friend.

After a moment, the voices calmed again, and she lay back down, pulling the covers over her, then turned onto one side and held a pillow, imagining that it was Angela, as she fell asleep.

"Good morning. Are you ready for your first treatment?" Angela asked Daniel the next morning.

Daniel was already seated in the rTMS, an ominous machine, resembling a mad scientist's version of a dentist's chair, which occupied the center of the room. "Yeah." His voice was tight.

"Don't worry. As I mentioned, this won't hurt at all. Now, please put these earplugs in."

Daniel took the plugs and looked questioningly at her.

"The machine can be a bit noisy." He inserted the plugs.

"Go ahead and close your eyes. This is going to take about an hour." Angela turned to the intern who had assisted Daniel. "Thank you. I've got it from here," she said, and the intern left.

She flipped a switch and adjusted a knob. A low hum filled the room, and Daniel winced. Angela adjusted the knob. "How does that feel?"

"My head hurts."

She turned the knob again, and his expression eased.

"Better?"

"Yeah."

For the first half hour of treatment, Angela cycled the machine through a set of treatment programs while gathering feedback from Daniel. This work fully occupied her mind and distracted her from her worries about Cassandra. However, Angela spent the second half hour of the session quietly monitoring the last program, the purpose of which was to make Daniel's brain more receptive to further treatments, and soon she was once again dwelling on Cassandra. She went back over the most recent dream-walking treatment, seeking clues to help unravel the mystery of Cassandra's voices and the nature of the shadow, but she got no further in understanding either. In her past experiences with therapeutic dream-walking, the nature of whatever was disturbing the patient became obvious, represented in the form of animals, humans, or plants, but in this case the dream-walk deepened the mystery.

When Angela finally switched off the machine and disengaged the coil, Daniel was asleep. "Daniel? We're done with the session."

As he opened his eyes blearily, she smiled reassuringly and

assisted Daniel to his feet. She tapped her ear, and he removed the earplugs and handed them to her. He cocked his head quizzically then grinned. "Doc, I think it's working. Something feels different."

Angela got out of the control chair and pushed the nurse call button. Picking up her clipboard, she scribbled briefly, then unclipped a form and handed it to him. "I'm glad to hear it. Do me a favor and fill out this evaluation form and give it to the nurse when you're done. After that, you're done for the day."

There was a knock at the door, and Ginny entered the room. "Dr. Cooper? Patient M is ready for his treatment."

Angela nodded. "Patient D will give you the evaluation when he's done." She turned to Daniel. "We'll do another treatment tomorrow at the same time. How's your room? Are you comfortable?"

"Hell yeah." He laughed. "Good food, pretty nurses. Can't ask for better."

"That's the spirit. We've got two more weeks with the trial. I have a feeling you'll be just fine." She left the room, thoughtful. Perhaps she should combine the use of the rTMS with dream-walking for Cassandra, she mused. She wasn't sure if the machine would interfere with the experience, though, so she filed the thought away for later consideration. She still had a full day of work ahead, with the final session scheduled with Cassandra, and she was filled with nervous anticipation.

The next two patients, a multiple personality and a drug addict who had had a psychotic break, were uneventful, and the initial results were already encouraging. Angela looked at her notes for patient F, her next patient in the trial. Frank Reynolds, age forty-two, homeless but in good health, was schizophrenic.

Ginny had finished prepping him for the machine, and he was in the chair waiting.

"Hi, Frank," Angela said cheerfully. "How're you feeling today?"

He was a beefy man, heavily tanned, and looked older than his years. His watery blue eyes focused on her for a moment and then flinched away. "Hey, Doc. I feel like Frankenstein."

She chuckled. "Well, don't go lurching off into the village and terrorizing anyone, okay?"

"Naw. Just tighten my bolts for me and I'll be okay." His fleeting smile was replaced by a hunted look.

Angela went over to the control panel and flipped a switch. The deep hum filled the room.

"Now, this isn't going to hurt at all. In fact, you might feel a tingling sensation." She sat on the stool. "I want you to tell me if you feel any discomfort, though, and I'll adjust it so you'll feel good."

Frank nodded and took a breath. Angela turned a knob, and the hum deepened.

"Yep. It tickles." Frank's left arm twitched, and Angela adjusted another knob until the twitching subsided.

"Okay, just relax, and we'll be done in just about twenty minutes. You can even fall asleep if you want."

Frank closed his eyes. Angela spent the next few minutes monitoring as the rTMS applied its oscillating magnetic field to Frank's brain. While she watched, her mind raced. Cassandra's problem had made her think once again of the time when she had used her dream-walking talent for therapeutic purposes. She had done so on behalf of gypsy patients and their relatives, those whom the system had tossed out rather than treat, and she had done most of her work in their homes.

When her grandfather had asked to help, she had at first demurred. Her therapy technique was intensely personal, and she had felt that having another person in the room would interfere, particularly a psychically gifted one like George. But his insistence that he would simply observe won her over. For about a year, he accompanied her on her surreptitious sessions, offering his observations afterward. With his help, she was able to test several of her theories, and she made significant progress in treating emotional disorders of many kinds. She had even considered going into private practice upon completing her internship, until the disastrous session with the Grey family changed her mind. Now that she had begun dream-walking with Cassandra, she felt renewed interest in the option of going into private practice in order to use her talent for healing.

There was a beep from the rTMS that jolted Angela out of her reverie. She reached over and switched off the machine, noticing with pleasure that Frank was sleeping peacefully. She touched him gently on the shoulder. "Frank, it's time to wake up."

His eyelids fluttered, and he groggily sat up. "Wow, I was out like a light." He looked at Angela with relief and broke into a full grin. "I feel great! This thing is fantastic." He hopped off the chair and stretched.

"Now, we'll schedule another session for you in two days as

part of the trial. In the meantime, take it easy, and drink plenty of fluids."

"You bet, Doc."

Angela got off the stool. "I'm going to send the nurse in to show you back to your room. Please fill out this questionnaire, and give it to her when you're done. I'll see you in a couple of days, okay?"

Frank stuck out his hand. "Dr. Cooper, thank you for this." His joy was genuine, and Angela realized that he was able to meet her gaze without flinching. This was a very good sign.

After she left the room, she notified the duty nurse and prepared herself mentally for the session with Cassandra.

LADDER UP

I
Breathe you
Into me
Open my hands
To give you safe space
My shadow is reaching
Hungry for your tender gift
I curve my back and hold you close
Tuck you into my secret warm place
You are safe there now, you are safe there now.
- C

6.

WHEN ANGELA returned from lunch, Cassandra had already clambered into the rTMS with Ginny's help, and a worried frown creased her face. Angela went to sit on the control stool and smiled at Cassandra. "How're you feeling today?"

"Okay, I guess." Cassandra grimaced in distaste.

"Did you sleep okay? Any nightmares?"

"No. How's this thing work?"

"This is called an rTMS. It is a harmless machine that re-trains the brain. We'll use it to help you tame those voices." Angela's tone was even and low.

Cassandra's frown deepened, but she said nothing. Angela reached over to the control panel, turned a knob, and adjusted the magnetic coil just behind Cassandra's head. The nurse handed her the clipboard with the treatment forms.

"Thanks, Ginny. I'll take it from here."

"Okay." Ginny smiled at the uncomfortable teen. "You're doing fine, Cassandra. I'll be back later." She left the room.

Angela waited until the door closed then quickly rose to her feet, crossed the room, and quietly locked it. She turned and looked back at Cassandra. "Are you sure you want me to be your chovihani? You need to trust me if you do."

Cassandra's face hardened. "You promised, Angela. I don't give a shit about this machine."

Realizing that it would be difficult to convince Cassandra to submit to the rTMS, Angela decided to keep it simple and avoid combining the two modalities. "We're not going to use the machine, but I have to run it to show use in the logs."

Cassandra nodded, though her expression didn't change. Angela went to the control panel and switched on the machine, and a low hum filled the room. However, she did not adjust the stimulation coil, but left it in the open position.

"Go ahead and lie back," she said. "We're going to go to the Otherworld."

Cassandra lay back down in the chair, looking steadily at Angela.

"Close your eyes. It's okay; I'll be right here."

Cassandra closed her eyes. Angela reached out and touched her forehead. "Now imagine that you're lying in a clearing in a forest..."

Angela felt the familiar sinking sensation of dream-walking, and the room blurred and dissolved around her to be replaced with the forest meadow under a daytime sky. Cassandra was lying in the grass, eyes closed, and Angela was seated by her side. All seemed calm, for which Angela was thankful. The scene rippled for a moment, lending it a sense of unreality. Cassandra's eyes opened, and she gasped in shock.

"Wha—Where am I?" She struggled to rise.

Angela got to her feet. Cassandra was entirely present with her in the Otherworld. Angela helped her to stand. The girl wiped her hands down her sides as if to verify her own reality. She looked at Angela.

"This place is real for you, right now. But it exists in your imagination when you're not here." Angela gestured at the forest. "Beyond this circle is your sleeping mind. All of your secrets and forgotten memories live there."

Cassandra shrank away from the trees and grasped Angela's hand. "It's quiet. Quiet and spooky."

"That's because when we started, you were calm. It's daytime because you're awake, too. But it's not really spooky, Cassie. What you see is inside you." Emphasizing the point, Angela touched Cassandra's head with the forefinger of her free hand.

Cassandra turned abruptly and hugged her. Angela patted the teenager awkwardly on the back and then disengaged, though Cassandra kept a grip on Angela's hand.

"For our first session, we need to explore the edge of this meadow. See?" She pointed at the dense, tangled undergrowth that was visible. "That stuff is what you've managed to push down below your consciousness most recently."

Cassandra scanned the woods. A small movement made her jump, and Angela felt her hand squeeze tighter.

"Yes. There are small creatures there. They can't hurt you, but they hold onto some of the pain that you need to face and release." Angela led her closer to the edge. The grass grew more luxuriant as they approached, and concealed in that grass were dead branches. A particularly tall patch of grass partially hid the picked bones of an animal.

Cassandra stared at the bones. "Stuff can die here? I thought this was... a dream place." She shivered.

"Dreams can die, too, can't they?" said Angela. "The ecology of the mind is every bit as real and meaningful as the ecology of the body." She tugged gently at Cassandra's hand. "Just a few more feet so we can get a close look at the edge of the forest."

They approached a patch of brambles that lay at the base of several gnarled trees. Angela noticed that the plants were armed with inch-long thorns and knew that Cassandra had some hard work ahead of her. She indicated the brambles. "This is where you've suffered a severe emotional setback. Whatever's on the other side can't get through. But I think we don't want to start here. The voices are obviously getting through somewhere else."

Angela scanned the woods again. She saw other thickets of brambles but no clearly defined paths. She led Cassandra along the periphery of the clearing while she explained what they saw.

"Here's a fallen tree limb. That's a near catastrophe from your past. Here... a rose bush. Nice! A friendship that's very meaningful to you. Let's see..." Angela stopped walking. They were at the edge of a boggy area, where the ground was saturated with water. Cassandra released Angela's hand and knelt by the bog.

"This usually signifies a powerful emotional release," she continued. Then she noticed that Cassandra's shoulders were shaking. She stood silently, giving Cassandra time to work through whatever the bog had triggered in her. While waiting, Angela looked around the meadow again. So far, she thought, there were no voices. This was very encouraging.

After a moment, Cassandra stood. She reached out for Angela's hand, and they continued. For the next half hour, Angela helped Cassandra to survey the territory of her mental and emotional landscape in the Otherworld. Twice they startled a small animal, and once Cassandra excitedly pointed out a hawk soaring above them.

"That hawk is a very good sign. Usually it means higher

awareness. You have a deeper part of yourself that offers intu-
itive guidance. That part can see further than your everyday
awareness, and you can cultivate your connection with it to
access that guidance." Angela sighed. "Okay. I think we've done
enough for one session."

"What about the voices?" Cassandra asked.

"For some reason, they haven't troubled you today. They
may come in cycles. This is not uncommon, though in your
case I'm surprised we haven't seen any sign of them at all."

Cassandra peered worriedly at the forest but said nothing.
Angela led her back to the center of the clearing.

"Now, to get back, we must look for a path. Usually I just
search the ground and I'll see a part of the floor of the physical
world." Angela scanned the ground then pointed. "There. See
that floor tile?"

Cassandra looked and nodded.

"Let's start with that."

Angela put her foot down on the tile, and more tiles became
visible. Cassandra followed her as they walked a few feet, and
with every step the woods faded. Finally, they found themselves once again in the treatment room, standing a few feet
from the rTMS. Angela noted that Cassandra had moved with
her, but filed that information away for later consideration. She
released Cassandra's hand and touched her shoulder.

"Why don't you get some rest? You've worked very hard. I'll
send in the nurse, and she'll take you back to your room and
get you whatever you need."

Cassandra looked at Angela, cool and distant again. "I need
the voices to go away. That was a nice trip, Angela. You've

proved you're a chovihani, but you still gotta help me." She leaned on the rTMS and idly swiveled the magnetic coil. "I'm not crazy, you know." She looked back up at Angela, and her eyes narrowed. "That thing was just watching us, but next time it's gonna attack. Be ready for it."

Angela was taken aback at the sudden change in Cassandra's demeanor but knew that this was not uncommon with some patients. "We'll have another session tomorrow. I will help you. I promised, remember?" Cassandra remained silent.

With a sigh, Angela picked up the clipboard, shuffled the pre-written questionnaire to the top, and placed it on the stool next to Cassandra. "Can you do me a favor and give this to Ginny when she comes in? It's a questionnaire that all of the patients in this trial fill out, and I've already filled it in for you. We're going to continue pretending to use the rTMS so we can keep you here at the hospital, okay?"

Cassandra nodded but made no effort to pick up the form. Angela pushed the call button and waited for Ginny. Cassandra stood, staring at her, until the nurse arrived. After giving Ginny a brief update, Angela left.

That evening, Angela was still working at nine o'clock, and she decided to eat at the hospital cafeteria rather than fight traffic just to get home late and still have to scrounge for food. The salad bar was decent, and earlier at lunch she had seen several slices of cold quiche that she hoped would still be there for dinner.

When she got to the cafeteria, it was nearly deserted, but she saw Ginny at one of the tables. She waved to her, went to the buffet with a tray, built her salad, and grabbed a couple of slices of the quiche. Angela made her way to Ginny's table and sat down.

"Lost your mind yet?" Ginny asked with a quirk of her mouth.

"Long ago. Don't miss it one bit." Angela ate a forkful of quiche.

Ginny finished her salad and started on a yogurt. "So, Eric emailed me and asked after you. Said you were, and I quote, in hiding, and that he hoped you were okay."

Angela rolled her eyes. "He thinks I'm like an older sister sometimes. A troubled, wayward sister." They both laughed.

"I told him you were working on the new trial. Then he said that you work too hard and need to go play." Ginny cocked an eyebrow at Angela and paused, holding a spoonful of yogurt.

Angela shook her head. "I'm close to a breakthrough with a very promising patient..."

"Patient C?" Ginny asked.

"Yeah, her. How'd you know?"

"She's gotten the lion's share of your attention." Ginny scraped the container empty and set it down. "So you think you can help her?"

Angela ate, collecting her thoughts. She wished she could confide in Ginny, but she could not risk the repercussions, both personal and professional, that would result from revealing her dream-walking talent.

"I think so, Ginny," she said finally. "She's responding very well to treatment. Haven't you noticed that she's less prone to violent attacks?"

The nurse cleared her throat and put down the spoon. "Actually, what I've seen is that when you're not around, she doesn't eat, and she just stares at the walls or writes her poems." She paused. "I think she's developing a transference projection."

Angela stared at Ginny. If she was seeing this, others were as well, and this could complicate her work with the troubled teen. As far as the rest of the hospital was concerned, Cassandra had to be no more than one challenging patient among many. This line of inquiry had to be stopped. "Thank you, Doctor."

"I'm serious."

"Well, so am I." Angela sat back in her chair. "I think I'd know when I'm dealing with transference and countertransference. And that's not happening here. If anything, Cassandra is releasing some very old attachments and making great progress here."

Ginny looked unconvinced. "Then how do you explain her behavior?"

Angela picked at her food and gathered her thoughts. "She is experiencing side effects from the treatment. There will be depressive episodes. You know the protocol accounts for that." She glanced up at Ginny. "And besides, it's only been a few days. Cassandra will settle down and show improvement soon, I know it."

Ginny looked doubtfully at Angela. "I hope so. That girl can't stand to lose an ounce. Listen, can we put her on a drip to get some weight back on those bones?"

"Do whatever you think is necessary to keep her in good

health. I really appreciate it. Let me take care of the mental issues." Angela smiled with relief. "Listen, when this trial is over, I'm going to take some time off. Do you think you can come out to the cabin for a weekend?"

"I'd love to! I'll arrange for a cat sitter. My neighbor's daughter has done a good job in the past."

"Great." Angela felt herself relax. They finished eating, chatting amiably, until Angela finally left for home.

The next morning, Angela scheduled Cassandra for treatment in the first available time slot. After wading through her backlog of messages, she left her office and walked down the corridor to the block of rTMS rooms.

"'Morning, Ginny," she said, as the nurse exited Cassandra's room. "How's patient C?"

Ginny handed Angela the chart. "She seemed cheerful this morning. She's ready for you now."

"Thanks." Angela went to the door, knocked lightly, then entered. Cassandra was sitting upright in the chair, and when she saw Angela, she smiled tentatively.

"How're you feeling today?" Angela asked.

"Okay."

"Did you sleep okay?" Angela asked. "Any nightmares?"

"I had this weird dream." She hesitated, frowning.

"Go on," Angela urged, as she went to the control stool and sat down with the clipboard in hand.

"There was this man. He was really tall, and I could tell he hated me."

Angela felt a thrill. This was what she was waiting for, and it was gratifying that she was getting results this quickly. "How could you tell?"

"Well, he didn't say anything, but he looked really angry. Then he swelled up really big, like a balloon? And turned black. I was afraid he was going to eat me." She looked quickly at Angela. "Don't laugh at me."

Angela kept her face expressionless. "I will never laugh at you, Cassandra. Ever."

Cassandra stared at her and appeared satisfied with what she saw. "Then you walked over to him with a really big needle and popped him. He exploded. It was gross."

Angela made notes on the chart. It was time to help Cassandra confront her demons. Perhaps later they could pursue a more conventional course of treatment to help the girl clear some of the other issues they had found yesterday. "Cassie, we're going to go find the voices where they live. Go ahead and relax."

Cassandra lay back in the chair, her eyes fixed on Angela.

"Close your eyes. It's okay; I'll be right here."

Angela reached out and touched her forehead. "Now, just as before, imagine that you're lying in a clearing in a forest..."

Soon they were both in the forest meadow under a daytime sky. Cassandra got to her feet immediately. Angela smiled and rose to stand by her side. "Today we're going to call on the voices and tell that stranger to appear." She spoke calmly, though her heart was racing.

"Are they... you know?" Cassandra looked around the edge of the clearing.

Angela gently disengaged Cassandra's hand. "In there? Yes.

It might be harder to see what they look like right now, but if we're lucky, you'll be able to hear them if you listen."

Cassandra started walking toward the woods, and as if on cue, a muted whispering passed like a momentary breeze. Angela heard a sharp intake of breath from the teenager.

"You've got to protect me." Cassandra's voice was tight with restrained emotion. She stepped back, turning to face Angela, and her expression was hard. "Why did my family have to die? And why did you leave me there?"

Angela sighed and lowered her head, pausing before answering. A cloud passed briefly overhead as she gathered her thoughts. Memories of that fateful night came rushing back, quite vivid here in the Otherworld, and she had trouble keeping her composure.

"I don't know. Your mother came to this place that night, hoping for answers. But something went terribly wrong. It was..." She hesitated. "It was partly my grandfather's fault, but mostly mine." Angela clenched her fists and then looked at Cassandra. "And I would never have left you if I'd known you were still alive." She opened her hands and took a deep breath.

"But this is about you," Angela continued. "You will need to make peace with the shadow to heal yourself."

Cassandra stared at Angela, shaking her head. Angela noticed that the daylight was dimming rapidly, and she looked up. The sky was cloudless, but the sun was not nearly as bright as it was when they had arrived, and a hint of darkness appeared over the treetops. Along with it, the whispering again became audible and then faded. Angela knew she only had a moment in which to prepare Cassandra to face her fear. She decided to teach the method for evoking the light of the soul that, she hoped, would help illuminate the source of the shadows that were rising in this place.

"Cassandra, listen," Angela tried to inject urgency into her voice. "Your shadow is a part of you. A part that you've rejected and that you need to reclaim."

Cassandra glared at Angela. "I thought you were going to make it stop. Not psychoanalyze me."

The whispering came again, and both Angela and Cassandra looked at the trees. Angela beckoned to Cassandra. "Cassie! Quick! Stand in front of me. Keep your eyes on the forest."

Cassandra hesitated and then hurried over to position herself in front of Angela. Angela took her shoulders. "Now imagine the light in this place is getting stronger. As if the sun were coming out from behind the clouds."

Cassandra frowned in concentration but then watched in wonder when the immediate surroundings began to glow as if she were indeed shining a light on them. She looked down, as if expecting to see her body shining. As the illumination around Cassandra intensified, the forest darkened further, and the voices grew louder. One of them, a male one, predominated. "Come to me. There is peace..."

Angela recognized the voice, but she could not remember where she had heard it before. She clasped Cassandra's shoulders more firmly. "Wait for the shadow to appear. You must confront it here."

A human figure became visible at the edge of the forest. Angela could not make out any details.

"You are the bridge," hissed the voice. "I have looked for you in so many faces."

Cassandra trembled, and Angela worried that she might go into convulsions. "Look at the face."

The crowd of voices faded, but the man's words grew louder. He sounded amused. "You cannot stop me with your tricks." He laughed softly.

To Angela's dismay, the face became clearer, as if magnified, and for a moment it resembled the man of her dream. Then it changed, and Roger's face stared back at her, grimacing. Angela felt Cassandra stiffen, and she jerked partially free from Angela's grasp, raising her fists and shaking them at the figure.

"Shut up! Go away! Leave me alone!" Cassandra shouted, her voice cracking.

The ground trembled, and the air brightened dramatically. Then the surroundings dissolved, replaced with the prosaic treatment room as they returned to physical reality. Cassandra sat up in the chair, straining against Angela's grasp, and Angela half stood to prevent her from falling out of the rTMS.

"Shut up!" Cassandra shouted again, and then she collapsed, crying hysterically.

Angela hugged her close and rocked gently. "You're back. You did it. You faced it."

Cassandra took several shuddering breaths. She pulled back a little and locked eyes with Angela. There was an electric moment, their faces nearly touching. Angela's heart lurched, and the moment passed as she disengaged from Cassandra and tugged her doctor's smock down to straighten it. Cassandra remained sitting in the chair, staring at Angela.

"Now..." Angela paused. "Tomorrow we'll go there again, and

this time you'll talk back to the voice, and you will make it your ally."

"I can face the voices," Cassandra looked searchingly at Angela. "Angela? I think I..."

Angela refused to meet her eyes, uncomfortable with the sudden attention. She retreated behind her professional facade, busying herself with the machine. She switched off the rTMS, and the hum disappeared. She turned several knobs on the control panel machine, gathering her thoughts, then turned back with a bright smile.

"There! We just completed a treatment." Angela touched Cassandra's shoulder. "The nurse will help you back to your room. Get some rest. You'll need it. We'll pick this back up tomorrow, okay?"

Cassandra reached up with her hand and clasped Angela's then nodded, eyes still fixed on Angela's face. Angela gently withdrew her hand, walked over to the wall, and pressed a buzzer. The door opened and Ginny came in.

"Let's continue the micro-doses. The treatment is going well, and I'll come back tomorrow to continue the initial phase."

"Okay. Is she going to need a glucose drip?"

Angela shook her head. "No, I don't think that will be necessary." She left the room without a backward glance.

Angela decided to spend a quiet evening at home, though that afternoon Eric had invited her to go out dancing again. Letting herself into the condo, she checked her voice mail on the smart phone and saw three messages. She knew that the first two were old messages from George, and expected the third to be also, as she had not returned his calls since his disruptive visit several days before. She clicked through the messages somewhat impatiently then played the last one for a moment.

"Granddaughter, this is important. We must talk. Please call me—"

Angela stopped the message, hesitated, and then erased them all. She went into the living room, extracted a bottle from her wine rack, uncorked it, and poured a healthy glassful of what she knew was a very good Californian Shiraz. She sipped, allowing the full-bodied flavor to roll around her tongue before she swallowed. Her eyes fell on a portrait of her and George out on a cruise aboard his wooden sailboat. She was at the wheel while he managed the lines amidships. Those were good times, when she was still an intern with high aspirations and confidence in her gifts, both intellectual and paranormal.

The wine was providing its intended effect, helping to ease the tension in her shoulders and put some of the stress of the day behind her. A sudden pang of nostalgia made her set her wine down, pick up her cell phone, and call George. The other end rang once.

"Hello?"

Hearing her grandfather's voice, she smiled. He had never gotten caller ID. "Granddad."

"Angel! You called me back! I did not think you would."

Angela sat in the chair next to the wine rack and picked up her glass. "Yeah. I didn't either." Unspoken was the plea that he would not make her regret reaching out to him. She knew he would pick that up, though. She sipped her wine.

There was a momentary pause. Then, "Angel, I know how you feel about me."

"Never mind that." He was already trying to manipulate her feelings, and it rankled her that it was working. "You said you had to tell me something."

She heard a soft grunt. "Yes. Yes, I do. It may be too much to ask, but can we meet?"

Angela shook her head. "No, we can't. We talk now, okay?"

"Okay. Angel, I know you have used your talent today. I could feel it."

Dammit, how dare he? Angela stood up and walked around the room. "That's none of your business. Granddad; you know how I feel about you snooping in my head like that."

"I was not in your head. When you go over, the world itself rings like a bell."

More of his nonsense. "What I do is a mind trick. Some kind of telepathy. Nothing more." He knew how she felt about the nature of her talent. She was sure he was going to start warning her, and that he was right to do so, though she would never admit it to him.

"Whatever you say, Angel. I am glad you have not turned your back on your gifts. But you are in danger."

Angela swallowed. Here it comes. She pretended not to understand. "What are you talking about?"

He sighed. "You must know, Angel. Whatever you believe, there is a shadow over you. I think I know what it is."

Angela stopped by the window and looked at the San Francisco skyline. How did he know about the shadow she saw in the morgue and on the dream-walks with Cassandra? A chill ran up her spine. "What about the shadow?"

"It is that same one that I saw over you that day when... when you were healing Esmerelda Grey."

She felt her breath quicken. "That's bullshit. There was no shadow! You touched me, and now the Greys are dead." She refused to tell George about Cassandra. "What I'm seeing now is an echo of my patient's trauma, nothing more. That's how my gift works."

"You do not know everything there is in this world. Angel, please listen to me!"

"No, I will not listen to your stories. Remember what happened the last time you started in with this talk about shadows?" Memories of the horror of that night, of the fire that killed the Greys, filled her mind.

There was silence on the other end. Angela could hear George breathing. Why couldn't he tell her something useful instead of offering scary stories from her childhood?

"If that's all you wanted to say to me, I've got to go. I've got a busy day tomorrow." There was further silence, so she punched the off button and set the phone down with an exasperated sigh. She picked up her wine, drained it without tasting it, then stood by the window, staring out at the night. She knew she would need to confront George soon. Evidently he knew something, but his ignorant Roma superstitions were coming between him and a rational understanding of what his perceptions were telling him.

After several more glasses of wine, Angela was able to go to bed.

"Dr. Cooper," said Angela, answering her office phone the next morning.

Josef Lindquist's tone was, as always, terse and clipped. "Good morning. Dr. Cooper, your clinical trial is getting some interest. Several specialists would like to observe your work."

This was bad news. Angela was beginning to make progress with Cassandra and could not afford to interrupt it for the sake of observers. "Dr. Lindquist, I don't think that's a good idea. The patients in the trial are vulnerable, and a new element could skew the results."

"I understand, Doctor, which is why I would like you to use an observation room. Your patients need not see anyone else."

Angela cradled her head in her hand. Having observers meant that she would be unable to dream-walk with Cassandra, as she had never found a completely reliable way to surreptitiously use her talent. Not only was physical contact not a part of the protocol she had designed, but in the recent dream-walks, she and Cassandra had "traveled," which would be very difficult to explain to anyone watching her work. She marshaled her arguments, though she knew they were weak.

"Everyone knows that the mirror is one-way glass. Several of my patients have paranoid symptoms. Josef, I don't think this is a good idea."

"Dr. Cooper, in this case I must insist. The clinical trial breaks ground in some very controversial ways. These observers are here to protect your interests and those of the hospital." His voice crackled with impatience.

Angela kept her voice low and steady. "The specialists can refer to transcripts and videos from consenting patients if they want more details than they'll get from the report. Josef, this is political interference."

"And I say that this is part of the protocol. Otherwise we shut down the trial."

Angela sighed. She recognized when Josef had made up his mind, and he could be stubborn and inflexible at times like that.

He continued. "I thought you'd be happy about this. These are the top names in the field. If they see positive results, it could transform the profession."

It was a devastating argument. Her original reason for designing the protocol, after all, had been that it would, indeed, revolutionize emergency psychiatry by accelerating the treatment of high-risk patients, with greatly reduced cost and minimal use of pharmaceuticals. She tried another tack. "I'm sorry, you're right. I will agree, but on one condition. I must be notified ahead of time if there are observers."

But Josef was ready for her. "Dr. Cooper, they would prefer that you do not know. This is essential to a double-blind protocol."

"Dammit, the protocol already incorporates double-blind procedures. Using an observation room is going to distort my findings. You know that."

"They don't know that, though. Okay, I'll talk to them. Maybe they can choose a small sample of patients. Would that be acceptable?"

She knew he was throwing her a bone, but she had to take what she could get. Josef rarely capitulated in situations such as this. "I guess it'll have to be. Please ask them to give me a list of patients for observation."

"Of course. Thank you, Dr. Cooper. I appreciate your coop-eration."

Cooperation my ass. She hated being condescended to like that. Angela hung up then smacked the desk in frustration. She picked up the phone again and made arrangements for a trial room with an rTMS machine and a gallery with ten chairs.

Angela hung up and sat for a few minutes, racking her brain for ideas. For the double-blind trial, the rTMS machines had been fitted with concealing panels to prevent her or any other researcher from seeing whether they were administering real or sham treatments, but she knew how they were designed. She believed she could rig the machine in the observation room so that when she was using it she could control whether it was active or not. Since she was still in charge of the trial, and none of the other researchers had questioned her insis-tence that she treat Cassandra herself, this ruse would probably work.

Satisfied with her plan, Angela left the office to begin the day's treatments. She didn't look forward to her patients' reac-tions to the one-way glass, particularly Cassandra's, but she would do her best to convince them that this was a necessary part of the treatment.

"Cassandra, we have to do it that way."

Cassandra glowered at Angela from where she sat, cross-legged, on her hospital bed. They had been arguing about the observation room for fifteen minutes, ever since Angela had come in to warn her. Now Cassandra refused to talk, and

Angela wondered how to break the impasse. With an exasperated sigh, Angela dropped into the visitor's chair. "Look, I've already told you. If you want my help as your chovihani, we have to change how we do things. I know; you think that their attention will weaken your resistance. But trust me when I say that we can still do this."

Cassandra muttered, looking down at her hands.

"Speak up. I can't hear you," said Angela.

"I said, this is what the shadow wants. It wants more people to see me."

"Why? Why would your shadow want people to see you?"

"It's not my shadow!" Cassandra glared at Angela again. Then her glare subsided into a haunted expression. "It's using you, Angela. Can't you see that?" She hugged herself and rocked slowly.

"Look, Cassandra. Cassie. If you don't agree to this, they're going to force you to move into an observation room anyway, and we won't be able to do any more dream-walks. My hands are tied. My boss..."

"The shadow is your boss now," Cassandra said in a dull voice. She looked up at Angela, and her eyes glistened with new tears. "The voices are coming back. Please. Help me."

Angela leaped out of the chair and over to Cassandra's bedside. "Quickly, lie down."

Cassandra awkwardly fell to her side, unwilling to unclasp her arms. She began shivering, on the verge of convulsing. Angela reached over and touched her forehead. Moments later, they were both on the grass in the Otherworld meadow. Angela could hear the whispering voices now, being attuned to Cassandra's mind, and she stood to survey the scene. The sky was overcast, and a wind was whipping the trees and making the grass hiss. Cassandra lay where she was, still hugging herself, though the trembling had subsided.

"Cassie, we're here. Look, I'm going to show you something you can do to stop the convulsions." She reached down and held out her hand for Cassandra to grasp. The teenager looked up at her and then unfolded an arm to take Angela's hand. She stood shakily but did not release her grip. The wind subsided, though the voices emanating from the woods around them were louder in contrast.

"Good. How're you doing?"

"Okay," Cassandra mumbled. Her fingers moved in Angela's grasp, and she squeezed the doctor's hand more firmly.

"Now, this is something I learned to do that was really helpful. Years ago, someone else I treated heard voices and had convulsions. He was a man about my age, and he was diagnosed with schizophrenia. What I want you to do is to concentrate on a spot on the ground in front of you."

Cassandra shook her head.

"Cassie, it's okay. Trust me."

The girl frowned, but then she lifted her head and stared at a spot about five feet away.

"Good. Now imagine that the spot grows in size until it's about six feet across. See it as if the grass were bent flat."

At first, nothing happened, but then Angela saw the grass tremble and lay flat in a rough circle. She beamed at Cassandra. "Great job! It took that guy a lot of tries to do what you just did."

Cassandra smiled shyly at Angela. "It wasn't that hard."

"Not for you it wasn't. Okay, now this can be tricky. Imagine that there are rocks just under the surface, and see them push up at the edge of the circle to make a ring."

The earth bulged immediately at the perimeter of the circle, and dirt-crusted rocks shouldered the grass aside. Soon there was a stone circle.

"Excellent. Now step into the circle."

Cassandra looked doubtfully at Angela, who disengaged her hand from the girl's. Then, tentatively, Cassandra stepped across the stone circle. Her mouth dropped open then, and she looked wonderingly at Angela. "The voices are gone!"

Angela could still hear them in the trees. "Really?" All she had expected was that Cassandra would feel calmer and stop convulsing. The disappearance of the voices had not happened with the schizophrenic patient. Perhaps this indicated that the voices were a manifestation of Cassandra's telepathic talent, and the stone ring represented her ability to shut them out. If so, then what was the shadow?

"Yeah." Cassandra twirled in place. "They're gone!" But then she stopped abruptly. "Wait. I can't do this without you." Her face fell.

"Yes, you can. Look at the ring and find a small stone. No bigger than your pinky finger."

Cassandra bent and scrabbled among the stones. She picked one up. "This big?"

"Yes. Put it in your pocket. When we get back to the hospital room, all you need to do is imagine that you still have that stone in your pocket, and when the voices come back, reach in and hold it with your hand. It will connect you to this place you've made."

Cassandra's eyes shone with tears of relief. Impulsively, she reached over and hugged Angela tightly. "Thank you so much. Thank you, thank you."

Angela squeezed then pulled back a bit. "There's a downside, Cassie. While you're holding the stone with your imagination, other people will think you're catatonic, so you have to find someplace private to do this. It's because you're walling off the convulsions, and this also makes your physical body unresponsive. I don't really know if this will also make the voices go away. The man I treated still heard them. He just didn't have those seizures anymore."

She looked around at the forest. While she had been speaking, the whispering had faded, and the clouds overhead were entirely gone. Bright sunlight filled the meadow with warmth.

Turning back to Cassandra, Angela smiled. "So, Cassie. Will you work with me? I showed you this trick, and we can do many other things together if you agree to let me treat you in the observation room."

"Angela, I'll do anything you want me to do." Cassandra's tone was happier than Angela had ever heard before.

"Okay." Angela gestured to the grass outside the circle. "Let's sit here. It's okay. The voices are gone now."

Cassandra stepped warily out of the circle, held still for a moment with one ear cocked, then settled down on the grass, kneeling and sitting back on her heels.

Angela sat. "What I'll do is pretend to treat you with the machine, and this time I'll lower the coil into position. I know how to set it up so it doesn't emanate any fields, but it'll still make noise. I'll touch you on the forehead as if to adjust your head position, and we'll be here."

"Won't they see us disappear?"

"No, it doesn't work like that. To them, we'll both look like we're sitting still, and you'll look asleep." She paused, considering whether to tell Cassandra about the times when she had seemed to disappear when those looking on had glanced away but decided against it. The watchers, if there were any for that session, would not all look away at the same time, and she hoped that if she and Cassandra didn't stray far that she wouldn't just get up and leave, or whatever it was that she did when she "disappeared."

"Let's just soak up some rays here," she continued, smiling. "I think you've done enough hard work for the day."

Cassandra looked startled. "It wasn't hard."

"Maybe it didn't seem hard, but trust me. You'll be exhausted when we get back. Making these constructs," Angela indicated the stone circle, "takes a lot out of the psyche. You can recharge your batteries for a few minutes here, but we need to get back to the hospital room really soon."

They lay back on the grass and enjoyed the warm sun of the Otherworld. Angela found that she had to struggle to keep her eyes open. All of the late nights and worry had drained her reserves, and she knew that she would pay later. On the rare times she had fallen asleep in the Otherworld, she had simply awoken in the physical world, but she was not sure if the same would be true for Cassandra.

She waited for a few more minutes, and then at her signal

both arose. Angela led Cassandra on a quick hunt for floor tiles, and they used those to return to her room. Cassandra was standing by the bedside and swayed on her feet, looking very tired.

"See what I said?" Angela helped her lie down. "Get some rest, and we'll pick this up tomorrow, okay? We'll do what we discussed."

Cassandra nodded sleepily and then rolled over onto her side and was soon snoring. Angela quietly let herself out of the room, taking her clipboard with her.

A Maze Ing

Mama makes me
Matter moves me
Mocking my misery
Why?
Love lifts life
Laughter lingers longer
Let light leave
Eh?
Dead did die
Denying defeats deeds
Done doing
Why?
Love!
- C

7.

TUESDAY MORNING, the observation room was dark and cramped, illuminated solely by the treatment area on the other side of the one-way glass. Josef had led the visiting specialists, Doctors Billings, Johnston, and Rivers, to the room. There were ten small, uncomfortable chairs, which were arranged in a horseshoe pattern, like a small operating theater, facing the one-way glass. The hot coffee and doughnuts on the side table were untouched, and the aroma made Josef's stomach grumble.

Rustling filled the room as the doctors folded back the paper on their clipboards. Several of them conferred quietly, and Josef saw with satisfaction that they were all keenly interested in the rTMS machine visible through the glass. Cassandra was already reclining in the chair while to one side Ginny wrote on her chart.

"Dr. Cooper should be arriving about... now," said Josef.

Dr. Cooper entered the treatment room, and Cassandra looked up at her. The doctor's footsteps sounded tinny in the speaker above the window. Ginny handed her the clipboard. "She's ready for you. Let me know if you need anything."

Dr. Cooper nodded. "Thanks. I'll do that."

Ginny left the room and shut the door quietly.

"Hi, Cassandra," said Dr. Cooper. "How're you feeling today?"

"Okay," Cassandra mumbled.

Angela took her seat at the control panel and adjusted several dials. She studiously avoided looking up at the one-way glass. "We're going to continue the rTMS treatment today. I think it's going very well, don't you?"

"I guess so."

Angela switched on the machine, and the low hum filled the room. "Okay, just relax and we'll get started."

She started to move the coil near Cassandra's head. The girl looked anxiously at Angela, who smiled to reassure her. "This won't take long, I promise."

Turning away from the glass, Angela crossed her fingers so only Cassandra could see them. Cassandra understood the gesture, and she nodded compliance, grinning. But then her grin vanished, and she looked up and around as her face twisted in fear.

"It's here! The shadow!" Her voice rose. "No. No. No." Cassandra levered herself up on her elbows and tried to clamber out of the chair.

Angela shook her head, her fingers still crossed. "Cassandra, no! Please, stay on the chair."

Cassandra swung her legs off of the chair and retreated to the far side of the room. Whispers came and went, and the lights dimmed. Angela glanced around the room and saw darkness crowding its corners. She shook her head. This couldn't be happening here, not in the observation room. If there was anyone watching, they would label her behavior as erratic and delusional if she responded to the shadow.

"Remember what we did last time? Cassandra, remember what I told you." Angela reached toward Cassandra, and two things happened. The lights went out completely for a moment, and a loud thud came from the direction of the one-way glass. Cassandra shrieked.

In the observation room, one of the specialists, Dr. Billings, was looking unusually pale and drawn as he leaned heavily against the one-way glass. He stood over his colleague, Dr. Rivers, who was crumpled on the floor. Josef rushed to the unconscious Rivers.

"Dr. Rivers! Are you all right?" He glanced up at Billings. "What was that all about?"

"So... hungry..." gasped Billings. "Bring me the..."

In the treatment room, Cassandra was leaning against the wall to the left side of the room and moaning. "Young one so I can... No..."

"... Feed," said Billings. "Feed me... You will..."

Josef and Dr. Johnston helped Dr. Rivers up. He was barely able to walk as they guided him toward the door. Billings ignored them.

"Someone call a nurse," said Josef. "This man needs help." He paid no further attention to what was happening in the treatment room or to the fact that Angela had apparently lost control of her patient. He would deal with that later.

Angela noticed that the room had become noticeably darker after the lights had come back on, and the vision of trees overlaid the walls. She gave up trying to get near Cassandra, who was cowering against the opposite wall of the room. Angela glanced worriedly at the one-way mirror; then she resolutely turned away from it and stared at Cassandra. She could not risk exposing her unorthodox methods to the visiting specialists, who she was sure were observing her. That thud was especially alarming, but she had to concentrate on what was happening in the trial room. In desperation, she tried reaching out to Cassandra's mind, using a method her grandfather had taught her that, unfortunately, she had never fully mastered.

Cassie? Cassie. Can you hear me? She spoke sub-vocally, moving her tongue without opening her mouth.

Cassandra looked at Angela's face and opened her mouth to speak, but then she clapped her hands to her ears and slid down the wall into a crouch. Angela tried again, more forcefully.

Cassandra. There was no further response. *Use the stone circle! Find the stone!*

Cassandra mumbled. "She can't hear you..."

In the observation room, Billings said in a low monotone, "... but I can. Your voice is sweet."

A nurse and an orderly assisted Rivers out of the room. Josef stood to one side with another of the specialists, Dr. Johnston, who was pale and gasping. Though another orderly was fitting Billings with padded restraints, he continued staring into the treatment room.

"We were observing Dr. Cooper when Billings just attacked Rivers," he told the nurse. Johnston tore his gaze away from Billings.

"He doesn't seem to be himself," said Johnston in a trembling voice.

"I can taste your fear," crooned Billings in a low voice, and his face seemed to blur for a moment. The orderly froze, staring at him. The lights flickered again, and the room filled with the stench of relaxed bowels.

Cassandra fell to the floor against the wall, partially curled in a fetal position. Angela circled around the rTMS machine and went to her side. She reached out to Cassandra, who at first shrank away from her touch. Then Cassandra collapsed into her arms, sobbing. Angela sighed with relief that the attack was over.

"C'mon, let's get up. We need to get you to your room."

The door opened, and Josef and Ginny entered.

"Dr. Cooper?" He was pale and appeared shaken. "There's been an accident."

"What do you mean?"

Josef passed his hand over his face, which still glistened with sweat. "I need to speak with you in my office."

"Okay." Angela turned back to Cassandra. "Cassandra, Ginny will help you back to your room."

Cassandra looked back at Angela with a stunned expression on her face. Angela smiled reassuringly at her then followed Josef out of the room as Ginny went to Cassandra's side.

"What was that all about?" asked Angela as they walked toward his office. Then, remembering the thud she had heard, it occurred to her that the accident Josef referred to was connected with the shadow haunting Cassandra. Her steps faltered as she felt a shiver of dread.

He shook his head, oblivious to her distress. "I'd rather not talk about it here. It's a liability issue."

The hallway was in a chaotic uproar with orderlies and nurses hurrying in every direction. Angela doubted that anyone would even notice them in all the confusion, but she said nothing.

They continued in silence until Josef ushered Angela into his office and closed the door behind them. Josef went to his desk and sat heavily in his chair. "Dr. Cooper, one of the specialists had some form of breakdown while in the observation room."

Angela opened her mouth to speak. Josef raised his hand. "Yes, you were being observed today."

"Breakdown? What do you mean?" Angela said. She was sick with worry over what had happened to Cassandra but hoped that Josef would mistake her distress for concern over the specialist. She began pacing then forced herself to relax and stood with her hands at her sides.

"We're not sure. Dr. Billings attacked one of the other specialists. Both he and the victim are in the ICU, but his prognosis isn't good. I would say that he experienced a psychotic break, complete with hallucinations and violent behavior."

Angela drew a hissing in-breath before she could stop herself. It was worse than she feared. Whatever was going on apparently did affect others besides her and Cassandra. She considered the possibility that George was right and an entity of some kind was responsible for the bizarre phenomena. This was beginning to look like something beyond her training and expertise, and for the first time in her life, she feared the Otherworld and what it contained.

Josef continued. "We're going to have to put the trial on hold."

Her head snapped up, and she stared at Josef. "What? Why?"

"This accident casts doubt on our facility. We don't know why this happened, and until we do..." He shook his head.

Angela looked around the room and waved to indicate the hospital. "How could we be considered responsible for this man's breakdown? He could have been under a great deal of stress, or he could have a health problem. Why do I need to pay a penalty for this incident?"

"You are taking this entirely too personally, Dr. Cooper. A rest might be a good thing for you, too. I have heard rumors..." Josef stopped and sighed.

Ignoring his insinuations, she placed her hands on Josef's desk and leaned over him. "If we put the treatments on hold now, I guarantee you the trial will be compromised. This work is very important for our hospital, not just for me, and you are taking a big chance here."

Josef shook his head. "This won't take long, I promise you. The patients will be kept here until we finish our investigation."

Angela threw up her hands. She could not afford even a day's interruption in any of her patients' treatments, but this was especially true with Cassandra. She felt that a break-through was imminent, and it was likely that she would be unable to visit the girl while the trial was on hold. "They're going to wonder what happened, you know. What do you think I should tell them?"

Josef opened one of the file drawers in his desk, searched the folders, and handed her one. "Here are the forms they need to fill out. You know what the hospital guidelines are, right? Tell your patients we're doing the work in phases. That's all they need to know."

Angela took the paperwork and flipped through it irritably. "I'm going to have to start over with some of them." Her mind raced as she tried to find some way out of the mess. "Look, I'm going to stay in the call room tonight. I've got a lot of catching up to do with the other subjects now."

Josef waved a hand. "Okay. I'll let you know if anything changes."

That night, after gathering her patients' forms and attending glumly to the paperwork, Angela ate her meal in the hospital cafeteria without really tasting it. She prepared the call room for an overnight stay, knowing that she needed to be nearby in case Cassandra had a crisis. Her instincts told her that if she left, she might lose whatever chance she had for helping the troubled girl.

She slept poorly on the lumpy bed, drifting in and out of consciousness and trying, unsuccessfully, to find a comfortable position. Some sound or a change in the air woke her suddenly. Her heart racing, she sat bolt upright as her eyes flew open. Angela found herself staring at the foot of the bed. Cassandra stood there in her hospital gown, shrouded in moonlight. Angela fought down a wave of terror as clammy sweat broke out all over her body. That was no dream!

Angela swung her legs off the bed, never taking her eyes off of Cassandra, whose own eyes appeared to be closed. "How did you get in here?" she said, her voice cracking. In a firmer voice, "Cassie, wake up. You're sleepwalking."

There was no response. Angela turned on the bedside lamp, stood slowly, and reached out to Cassandra, preparing to waken her. She hesitated, another chill running down her spine, when she saw that the pale aura she mistook for moonlight clung to Cassandra's body in the darkness. She slowly withdrew her hand as Cassandra turned her face toward Angela, though her eyes still closed.

"Angel. You freed me. In my dream," said Cassandra in a strangely familiar, deep voice.

"Roger?" Angela's head swam with dizziness. It could not have been him, but the voice was so much like that of her dead patient. She took a shuddering breath and tried to get her reactions under control.

"Cassie, please wake up." There was no reply, but Angela was determined to treat the situation at face value. To do otherwise was to descend into horror, and she would not allow herself to lose control. "Okay, then. I'll get an orderly. We'll take you back to your room."

Angela pressed the call button on the wall and then gingerly reached out to grasp Cassie's upper arm. She gasped when she touched it. It was cold, rigid, and impossible to move. Cassandra looked down at Angela's hand, and Angela saw that her closed eyes were streaming with tears that flowed freely and splashed on the floor. Angela looked down and saw a line of puddles. There was no way for that to have come out of any human tear ducts. She glanced back up at Cassandra's face as she released her arm and stepped back involuntarily. Cassandra's face and form had changed. She was dressed in tattered rags, and her face seemed to have aged dramatically.

"What the hell?" Angela could not keep her voice from quavering.

Cassandra's eyes opened. The tears were twin rivers flowing down her cheeks. Her mouth opened, revealing toothless darkness. "I'm a poet," she said in a cracked voice. "Mama told me that. She said all art is one, and I am the greatest artist who ever lived."

Cassandra's aura had brightened, and the room had darkened in contrast. It was a spontaneous dream-walk, she realized. That would explain the surreal shifts in Cassandra, though Angela still did not know what might have brought the girl to the call room and why she looked the way she did. She glanced around, looking for the telltale clues that would show her the way back to physical reality.

"I have returned and lack only your gift." It sounded like a crowd of people had spoken. Angela whipped her head around. Cassandra's eyes glowed with power, but then they flickered, and she blinked. With a grunt, the girl shrunk into the form of the child that Angela had met in the first dream-walk. In a high, piping voice, Cassandra said, "Mama? Where am I?"

Angela's clinical mind kicked in, and she felt calm wash over her. She realized that the appearance of the child offered a very important clue to heal Cassandra and help her reintegrate her shadow. If she could communicate with the regressed form of the girl's mind, it was possible that she could bridge the divide between her past and present selves and heal her.

"Cassie, I'm here." Angela was half crouching with her hands on her knees. "You're in my room. Listen to my voice. My voice is all you hear."

Cassandra stared up at Angela, her eyes glistening. "Yes, Mama."

Angela once again grasped Cassandra's arm, which was now child-sized and no longer rigid. "You are a poet. You write beautiful poems, Cassie. Have you always been a poet?"

The little girl looked down shyly. "Yes."

"Do you love to write?"

More quietly. "Yes."

"What are your poems about?"

Cassandra kicked one shoed foot with another. "They're about people, and animals, and trees, and about me. Mostly me." She looked up at Angela. "Mama says my poems are windows of my... my..."

"Soul?"

"Yeah."

"I see now," Angela said. And she did. Cassandra's pain of loss had buried the joy she expressed in her poetry. Those writings held the key to her recovery. Angela was certain of that. "Cassie, let's go back to the real world."

Angela peered at the ground, looking for markers such as floor tiles or a path. She started to take a step but stumbled as she realized she could not move her feet. She looked down at them and gasped in horror when she saw that disembodied hands had reached up from the ground, holding her firmly. Her vision dimmed, and her gaze was dragged back up to stare as Cassandra once more changed into the very tall woman of her dreams. She jerked back in shock and fell heavily into darkness.

Angela awoke. She was on the floor with the iron taste of blood in her mouth. Her tongue was bitten and swollen, and when she staggered to her feet and turned on the light, she saw that she was alone in the room. She went to the door and opened it cautiously, but as she expected, she saw no one in the darkened hallway. She walked unsteadily to the call room's bathroom and switched on the light. In the mirror, her own haggard, bruised face looked far worse than she would have expected from a simple fall. *What the hell happened to me?*

She had had many spontaneous dream-walks when she was younger, but they had stopped years ago, only resuming when Cassandra had shown up. Obviously something momentous had just happened, and she decided that she could not wait until morning to find out what it was. As Angela left the call room to check on Cassandra, the night-shift orderly at the security station saw her and gasped.

"Dr. Cooper?" he said. "Are you okay? What happened to your face?"

"I'm okay. I just tripped. Need to look where I'm going." Angela suppressed a grimace, hoping he would let it drop.

Okay." He frowned, but her air of authority dissuaded him from pursuing the subject further. Angela proceeded to Cassandra's room.

Angela opened the door to Cassandra's darkened room and entered, locking the door behind her.

"Cassie?" she murmured. "Are you awake?"

"Yeah." Cassandra's voice trembled. Angela turned on the light and saw Cassandra sitting up in bed, hugging herself.

Angela walked to her side. "Do you know what just happened?" She wanted to touch Cassandra's shoulder but was worried that it would frighten her.

"I had a nightmare—"

"I know," Angela said, interrupting her. "I was there, too. Remember?"

"I... Yeah. I think so."

Angela sat on the side of the bed. "Do you have another poem for me?"

Cassandra stared at Angela in confusion, but then she turned to her bedside table and pulled out a spiral notebook. Wordlessly, she handed it to Angela, who flipped to the last written page. She scanned it then reread it slowly, nodding to herself.

"I thought so. This is what I needed to know. Go ahead and lie back down. We're going to try something. I think it'll help."

Cassandra slowly lay back, and she looked up at Angela with a simple, childlike expression on her face, fear smoothing away most of her years. Angela reached over and touched her forehead. The room immediately dissolved into darkness, and Angela stood in Cassandra's familiar forest clearing. It was a heavily overcast day, and Angela knew that it reflected the girl's emotional state. Cassandra was with her, clinging to her, and Angela gently disengaged.

"Okay, I want you to stand right here in front of me and look at the forest edge."

Cassandra mutely complied.

"Now, go back in memory to that day when George and I were at your house, visiting your mother."

Cassandra sighed when she saw herself as a child coming out of the forest. The child Cassandra was angry, with balled fists down by her sides and a thunderous frown.

"What did you do to Mama?" the child asked sharply.

Cassandra shook her head and shuddered. "I didn't do anything." Then she started sobbing. "I didn't do anything!"

The child raised a clenched fist and shook it. "Give me back my Mama!"

Cassandra said weakly, "I can't."

"I'm gonna kill you!" Now the child Cassandra was crying, and her face was red as she glared at her teenage self.

Angela heard whispering from the forest, and she resisted the urge to look for the source. Without warning, teenage Cassandra's legs buckled, and Angela caught her and helped her into a kneeling position. The girl was crying with great, gulping sobs. "Mama. Why did you have to die?"

The child screamed and rushed at them both, and she tried to pummel the older girl with her little fists. Cassandra caught her younger self and hugged her. The child struggled briefly and then dissolved into weeping.

Remembering what she had deciphered in Cassandra's latest poem, Angela murmured, "My Lady Love."

Cassandra, teen and child, gasped as one, then they blurred and dissolved into each other. Cassandra looked over her shoulder at Angela, her tear-dampened face transfigured by adoration. Angela felt as if a heavy burden had lifted from her shoulders, and she stood straight. Then the air shifted, and she heard a deep voice echo in the air. "Mine. All mine."

At that moment, a golden crackling aura appeared over Cassandra, floated for a moment, and then was drawn up into the air in a swirling vortex. Angela looked up and saw a circle of impenetrable black hovering overhead. The aura vanished, and Cassandra's eyes closed as she collapsed at Angela's feet.

"What the hell?" Angela gasped as a heavy blow struck her between the shoulders, and she fell to her knees and sprawled partly over Cassandra's body. A great wind arose, whipping the trees into a frenzy. A giant laugh echoed around the clearing, and a weight settled in Angela's mind, crowding out her sense of self. She rose on one arm and lifted the other above her in defense.

"Get out of my head!" she shouted.

A bright flash, like lightning, lit the clearing. There was a thick, quiet moment, with every sound muffled. Then there was peace. The trees abruptly became still, and the darkness faded. Angela fought against losing consciousness as she lay on the ground. Mustering her strength, she struggled to her feet, noticing that Cassandra was still unconscious. She breathed heavily, surveyed her surroundings, and bent to touch Cassandra, who abruptly vanished. Then the Otherworld disappeared, and Angela was once again sitting on the bedside beside a sleeping Cassandra.

"My God," she groaned, clutching her pounding head. "What just happened?" She reached down and tapped Cassandra. "Cassie, wake up."

Cassandra moaned then opened her eyes. She was trembling and obviously exhausted.

"It's gone, Cassie. It's okay." Angela helped Cassandra struggle to a sitting position.

The girl stared at Angela then looked around the room in confusion. "Where is everybody?"

"What do you mean?"

Cassandra looked back at Angela, her eyes wide. "I can't hear anything. All the voices are gone."

Angela searched her face and saw a new calm. "I think it worked," she said, wonderingly. She rose, unlocked the door, and stuck her head out into the corridor. "Ginny? Can you give me a hand here?"

After a moment, Ginny emerged from the night-duty station and came over with a questioning look on her face.

"Why don't you give Cassandra a checkup and get her some electrolytes. I need to file a report. And get me some painkillers." She pressed her hand against her head.

"Angela, are you okay? You look like someone beat you up!"

Angela shook her head gingerly. "I'll be fine. I just need to finish my beauty sleep."

Frowning, Ginny said, "Okay." She gestured at Cassandra. "Will she need medication?"

"No, I don't think she will." She turned back to Cassandra, who was still staring at her. "Cassie, I'll be back to check on you later, okay? I want you to get some sleep tonight. I think we made great progress."

Cassandra nodded, yawned, and lay down on the hospital bed.

"I'll see you both later this morning." Angela left the room. She couldn't remember how she got back to the call room, but when the door swam into view, she opened it, went to the narrow bed, and collapsed.

8.

THE CORRIDORS of the hospital at night were quiet, yet a tension could be felt in the old masonry. Pain and grief had been driven into the stone over the years, and the energy of those emotions was being reawakened by otherworldly influences. Old fears, bogeymen of disturbed minds, regained a vibrant potency, and the hypersensitive patients became infected by those fears. Anger, likewise, cast its red cloud over the minds of patients and staff alike, causing tempers to flare and old resentments to swell into new sources of irritation.

Deeper still were the evanescent hallucinations that, over time, had accumulated like astral debris in the dark corners and dusty corridors of the place. The pressure building in the Otherworld pushed the phantasms toward the waking minds of those for whom the corner of the eye was a source of terror. The nighttime shouts and daylight clamoring of those burdened with delusion caused no end of frustration for hospital staff.

For those already afflicted with "voices," buried screams and desperate pleas of past inmates overwhelmed the usual inner chatter creating a growing cycle of cacophony that threatened the sanity of everyone.

When Jane Doe was picked up in a routine sweep of the homeless in Golden Gate Park, she began screaming, clawing, and biting. Three burly officers immobilized her and transported her to the emergency ward at Franklin Psychiatric Hospital. By the time she arrived, she had quieted enough that restraints were no longer necessary. She calmly explained that the voices had commanded her to stay in the park overnight, threatening to kill her if she did not comply, which was why she had fought the officers.

Diagnosed with schizophrenia, she was placed in a seclusion room for observation. She would be released the next day with a prescription for antipsychotics, which was covered by Medicaid. However, tonight she had new trouble to contend with.

In her darkened room, Jane sat upright in bed, though she remained fast asleep. She had been resting peacefully under the influence of the mild sedative haloperidol, but in the last few minutes, she had experienced a chaotic panoply of dreams. Her closed eyes had begun darting back and forth, as if she were frantically seeking escape, and her breathing had become rapid and irregular. Then, in one convulsive movement, she thrashed into a seated position. Calm again, but with closed eyes and sleep-slackened face, she stared in the direction of Cassandra's room, awaiting instructions.

"Fuck you! Fuck! Fuck!" shouted the nude man on Market Street at noon that same day. Passersby gave him a wide berth, and he attracted a fair share of glares. He screamed racist imprecations and fondled himself repeatedly, until police officers arrived to throw him to the ground, cuff him, and wrap him in a blanket. They hauled him away to Franklin, and after being restrained and processed, he was placed in seclusion. John Brinks was a regular at the emergency ward and had a habit of throwing his medication away and continuing to make a public nuisance of himself.

He was scheduled to be released with a newly filled prescription the next day, but that night, he stood in his seclusion room. His sleeping mind was troubled with fantastic visions of dark forests thronged with restless spirits, and over all of them loomed a shadow that spoke and bestowed fantastic visions.

The standing man turned his head to stare in the direction of Cassandra's room.

Alan, a night-shift orderly, assisted Nurse Debra Williams, who struggled to administer a sedative to a thrashing patient in a padded seclusion room. Silence descended as the patient went slack and nearly fell off of the gurney. Alan, adjusting the patient's limbs, did not notice that Debra was no longer actively helping. "Deb, I've got him strapped in—" he began, but then he stopped talking. Both patient and nurse were staring silently at the wall. He did not know that they stared in the direction of Cassandra's room.

Angela slept the remainder of the morning in the call room. When she finally arose and opened the door to check on the day's activities, she noticed that the hospital looked busier than usual. There was a lot of shouting in the background, and harried nurses and orderlies were rushing with more than the usual urgency.

After splashing her face and brushing her teeth, Angela went to the nurse's station, dodging two gurneys wheeled at high velocity, to schedule the day and arrange to meet with

Cassandra. She had to wait several minutes for one of the nurses, and at one point, after signing a release form and nearly losing the skin of her knuckles when the clipboard was snatched away, she said to no one in particular, "What the hell is going on here?"

One of the passing orderlies said, "Something's gotten into the patients in this ward. We can't keep 'em sedated!" He vanished into the bedlam.

Angela saw Josef strolling amid the chaos and not giving a second look to the hospital staff, who were dashing in all directions. He saw her, smiled, and approached with a leisurely gait.

"Dr. Cooper! Good morning."

She stared at him incredulously. That could not be old stick-up-the-ass Josef, could it? "Good morning? What's good about it?"

His smile widened. "Great work with patient C. I just saw your report."

Angela knew that she had not filed a report yet, as she had just awakened, and she felt a momentary dizziness at the increasing surreality of the situation. "What report? Never mind." She gestured at the confusing activity around them. "This place is in an uproar, and the moon isn't full for another week. Doesn't that concern you?"

Josef shrugged. "It's always busy this time of day. Listen, I'm going to call a meeting later today to discuss expanding the trial and adding staff."

Angela shook her head in disbelief. "Can we do that another day? I've got my hands full here."

Josef's smile became a slight frown. "Make time today, please. The specialists are anxious to hear about your recent successes."

Angela threw up her hands. "Okay. When is the meeting?"

"How about four p.m.?" His smile was restored. "See you then, and thanks again, Dr. Cooper."

Josef strolled away, not giving a second look to the rushing nurses and orderlies. Angela shook her head again then turned back to the nurse's station. She spent the next fifteen minutes attempting to arrange a workable schedule for herself that included a check-in with Cassandra, then, after swigging a cup of water and a couple of paracetamol capsules, she returned to her office to catch up with the ever-present paperwork before making her rounds.

Margaret LaSalle had been working at Franklin for eight years as a nurse in the emergency ward, but she had never seen anything like what she saw that day. The only term for it that she could think of, unfortunately, was "madness," and she was at a loss to explain why so many patients were having simultaneous psychotic episodes.

Her shift started early when two male patients became violently belligerent and began threatening staff outside their seclusion rooms. Neither had been troublesome before, and their doors had been left unlocked, but now Margaret had to call the hospital police. When she did, however, she was told that they were already deployed elsewhere. Consequently, it was up to Margaret to recruit several orderlies to wrestle the men to the floor to allow her to administer an intramuscular sedative.

After restraining the men in their beds, or as she would say, "putting 'em in points," she began her normal rounds. Her day proved anything but normal, though, as every patient was impossible to treat without restraints or sedatives. It did not seem to matter what their diagnosed condition had been; as far as she was concerned, they had all become violent psychopaths.

The day was half over when Margaret felt a terrible burst of pain in the back of her head, as if someone had struck her with a heavy object. She had to sit for several minutes, cradling her face in her hands, until the headache abated. The migraine-like attack was repeated three more times in the next two hours, so as soon as she could, she took a systemic painkiller.

As she was attempting treatment of a patient with multiple personality disorder who had become completely unresponsive to sedatives or other medication, she saw Dr. Cooper leaving a seclusion room. Margaret hurried over to ask for help. "Doctor, I have a highly resistant patient. It's Carl. Can you advise me?"

Dr. Cooper thrust her clipboard into the hands of a waiting orderly and ran her hand through her hair. "Okay, I've got three minutes."

Margaret led her to the treatment room. Hearing a man shouting, the doctor threw the door open.

"He's coming! In the dreams! He's coming!" Carl was raving. Though he was restrained, he continued to struggle, and veins were standing out in his reddened forehead. As they entered the room, he turned bloodshot eyes in their direction. When he saw Dr. Cooper, he took a deep breath and let out a howl of anguish. She hurried to his side and glanced at the chart. The doctor muttered something then turn to face Margaret.

"Nurse, I need you to go outside and wait for me. Please, no questions. I think I can help this man."

At that moment, Margaret nearly collapsed as another migraine drove needles of pain through her eyes into her skull. She gasped and then stood panting as the pain passed through her head, down her neck, and along her back. When it reached her tailbone, it flared into a pulse of heat that made her yelp in shock, as a completely different sensation shook her frame.

When she looked up again, she saw that Dr. Cooper had not noticed her attack. The pain had mysteriously evaporated, leaving behind a slight euphoria and a throbbing sensation behind her eyes. Margaret left the room and continued her rounds, promising herself that she would consult a physician as soon as she could take the time.

Carl stopped howling when Margaret left the room, and he stared at Angela with a terrified expression. She reached out to touch his forehead, but he twisted violently away and began breathing in great, shuddering gasps. She had never tried to dream-walk anyone who resisted her so strenuously and was afraid to do so with Carl. However, she couldn't think of any other way to learn what was happening to him.

"Carl, listen to me. I hope you can hear me. I will not hurt you. I am here to help."

Carl was weeping with fear, and his eyes alternately darted around the room and focused on Angela. He was obviously beyond reasoning, so with a muttered prayer to whatever gods watched over fools, she reached out and, with some difficulty, managed to grasp the top of his head with one hand and gingerly touch his forehead with the other. Immediately, the room spun around her, and she felt a surge of nausea. The vision of trees appeared, but they were violently bent, and the earth shook beneath her feet. Angela concentrated on keeping her balance and holding down the granola bar she had eaten earlier that morning. Then, to her horrified ears came a thundering voice that she recognized all too well as belonging to the shadow.

"I am death and pain and hell! Fear me, creature of mud, and feed your soul to me."

The earth beneath her feet had not quite solidified, and now great crevices opened up all around her. Angela dropped to her knees, with her palms on the ground to steady herself, and looked up at a turbulent cloudscape strobed with lightning. She gasped with pain as a stone struck her on the shoulder. Then she crouched, arms over her head, as a storm of stones fell all around her, some striking her with jarring force. She could not think of anything except to get out of there, but there was no way for her to look around for any telltale markers from the physical world. Then, the ground heaved convulsively, throwing her into the air as a gigantic thunderclap deafened her.

Angela, stunned, came to herself on the floor of the treatment room. She expected to find bloody bruises on her arms and legs from the stones, but there wasn't a mark on her. Cautiously, she rose to her feet and looked over at where Carl was lying. He was still, and the silence in the room was ominous. Angela went to check his pulse and was not surprised to find that he had died. His face was twisted in a rictus of fear, and she reached over to close his eyes. Angela sobbed for a moment, overcome with exhaustion and despair, but she took a deep breath. Whatever was happening, it was clearly related to her work with Cassandra, and it was her responsibility to find its cause.

Pushing the call button, she informed the duty nurse of Carl's passing. Then, after leaving notes on his chart, she left the room to see to her other patients, dreading what she might find but determined to do what she could to help them.

Angela hurried down the hall to check on Daniel, who had been her most successful rTMS patient thus far. His room was next to Cassandra's, and she was worried that whatever had happened to the rest the hospital might have hit him especially hard. As she approached his room, she noticed that the door was open. Heart sinking, she rushed over. In the room were several nurses and a beefy orderly, and Daniel was strapped onto a gurney, hooked up to an IV, and looking very pale. A crash cart had been brought into the room.

"Daniel! What's happened?"

"He went into cardiac arrest a few minutes ago," one of the nurses replied. "We don't know what caused it yet, but we're taking him to the ICU." She and one of the orderlies got the gurney moving. Angela stood to one side as it was removed from the room then followed them out.

Walking alongside the gurney, she saw that Daniel's eyes were half open. "Daniel, are you awake?"

His eyes shifted to focus on her, and to her relief, he smiled, though the smile was somewhat strained. "Hey, Doc. I guess I'm not checking out, huh?"

She patted his wrist. "We'll find out what happened and fix you up. Do you remember anything?"

They were turning a corner into another corridor, and his forehead wrinkled in concentration. "I just had breakfast, and I was watching something on the tube." He stopped.

"Go on."

"You'll think I'm crazy." He laughed then winced. "Ow."

"Take it easy. If you're not up to it, you can tell me later." Angela regretted disturbing him, but her anxiety drove her to get answers if at all possible.

"No. It just hurts to laugh."

They got into an elevator, and Angela crowded in with the orderly and one of the nurses.

Daniel spoke again. "The room got real dark all of a sudden, like there was a cloud passing over outside, but then it looked like there was someone standing at the foot of the bed. It was a guy, I think. He was really tall, and he just stood there for a minute. Then he started talking. I can't remember what he said, but he scared the living crap out of me, Doc. And now here I am."

Angela felt a chill. Unlike Carl, who had been driven to full-blown psychosis, Daniel had not suffered so much mental harm. Obviously, Daniel had seen the man (or whatever it was) who had been haunting Cassandra and her, and that entity had tried to take his life. But why? She decided to check on Cassandra immediately, even though the girl had seemed to be in excellent condition when she left her with Ginny.

"Okay. Listen, I don't doubt what you saw looked real, but I suspect that your mind was throwing up an image to stop you from getting well. This happens sometimes. You'll get through it, I promise."

He smiled, though his eyes were tired. "Thanks. I think I believe you."

When the elevator doors opened, Angela got out. "Daniel, the nurse will see to it that you're taken care of in ICU. I expect to see you back on your feet and ready to go real soon, okay?"

"Sure, Doc."

Angela headed back to Cassandra's room, taking the stairs two at a time.

On the way up to her ward, Angela's pager beeped, and when she saw that it was a call from security, she took a quick detour to her office. As soon as she walked in, she called the number and found herself explaining to a disbelieving hospital security officer what had happened since last night. "Half the ward is under sedation. We're fighting to get it under control." The officer promised to send anyone he could spare.

Angela hung up and put her head in her hands, exhaustion already setting in. There was a knock on the door.

"Come in."

Ginny poked her head in the door. "Angela, the network just crashed. I couldn't page you. Can you come see Cassandra?"

Angela got to her feet, all tiredness forgotten. "That's weird. The HPs just paged me a minute ago. Yeah, I was on my way there anyway."

She followed Ginny to Cassandra's room, Angela fearing the

worst, but she was relieved when she saw Cassandra sitting up in bed. Her relief became concern again when she noticed that Cassandra did not turn her head when they entered the room but continued staring with a vacant expression at the wall.

"She's verbally unresponsive," Ginny said as they went to Cassandra's bedside. "I'd say shock, but her stats look normal."

Angela checked Cassandra's pulse and examined her eyes. She turned to Ginny. "She was okay when we finished the treatment yesterday. Did we change her meds? Anything?"

"No. The duty nurse found her like this. She is able to follow direction but doesn't speak or otherwise react."

Both jumped when they heard a shout, followed by a crash, from the corridor outside. Angela and Ginny hurried out of the room to see a mess in the hallway. Margaret was sprawled, unconscious, with a tray upended on the floor. Its contents were scattered, and some food had splashed on the wall. Several other staff members were attending to her, and Phil, one of the orderlies, looked up at Angela and Ginny as they approached.

"What's happened here?" Angela asked.

"I don't know," Phil said. "One moment she's taking a meal to one of the patients, the next she's on the floor."

One of the nurses checked her vitals. "Pulse is thready and weak. She's in shock."

Suddenly Margaret kicked and spasmed. Phil grimly hung onto her. One of her flailing arms delivered a resounding slap to another nurse, who was thrown against a wall and fell, stunned.

"She's convulsing. Sedative! Stat!" Phil took a loaded hypo

from Ginny. He expertly administered it, and then Margaret calmed immediately.

"Get her to an examining room," said Angela.

Margaret's eyes snapped open. "Soon I will have you, too..."

One of the assisting nurses said, "My Angel."

Margaret slumped. The other nurse groaned, "God! I've got a migraine." She put a hand to her head.

Angela's jaw dropped. The shadow! It was speaking through the hospital staff. Any remaining doubts she had concerning what her grandfather had told her vanished. She stepped back for a moment to regain her composure. *This has got to stop.* "Phil, get something for her headache. Get Margaret to the ICU, and let's get this mess cleaned up."

Angela stayed long enough to see that some semblance of order was restored, and then she went back to Cassandra's room. Locking the door, she went to her bedside and checked her vital signs again.

"You were doing so well." Angela sighed. She reached out to touch Cassandra's forehead, bracing herself for another wild ride. The clearing smoothly formed around her with no sign of the kind of trouble she had had with Carl, but it never fully solidified. That had never happened before, and mystified, Angela waited several more minutes. She remained standing by the bedside, gazing at the wavering, translucent trees beneath a watery blue sky, until she reluctantly lifted her hand. The scene vanished abruptly. She swore under her breath, wondering if there was something wrong with her. It was possible that Cassandra's unresponsive, seemingly comatose state created a barrier that prevented Angela's normal access, but all she could do was speculate.

"Cassie, I don't know if you can hear me, but I'm going to get some help for you. For all of us. I'm going to ask George for his advice. I will be back to check on you." She leaned over to touch her lips to Cassandra's forehead. She squeezed Cassandra's hand and left the room.

Under the clear blue sky, the hospital was a massive beast of stone that gripped the earth with columns and foundation stones. It no longer slumbered peacefully in the heart of the city, but squatted patiently, awaiting the arrival of its Master. He promised satisfaction for the hungry ghosts who gnawed perpetually at the warm lives within, and he promised wakefulness for the spirit of the place that had given the hospital its aura and its mood over the years.

Indistinct voices came from inside the building.

"Though you cast me out, I forgive you. Join me..."

"... and become one with me. Give me your gift..."

"... and we will shine upon this dark world again. Come, beloved..."

"... and rest in my arms. These children are ours to take."

James McTavish, an experienced orderly who worked in the psych ward at the hospital, had always thought of himself as the sanest man in the room. His coworkers often remarked that Buddhism was good for him, and they envied his calm in the midst of chaos. In fact, his Mindfulness training classes had become very popular with both staff members and the more tractable patients. But now his Buddhism had abandoned him, along with his mind, as he thrashed in convulsions on the floor. "Ours to take. Aaaah!" James went limp. Then his eyes opened, and he stared vacantly at the ceiling as a tear trickled down his cheek.

9.

ANGELA WAS about to call George when she received a page requesting her immediate assistance with several of the patients in the long-term care ward. She spent the next fifteen minutes administering sedatives and helping doctors with diagnoses and, in several cases, the transfer of patients to the emergency ward for urgent care.

At the next lull in the work, she went to a nurse's station to page Ginny over the intercom. She told her to initiate a lockdown in the emergency ward and send notice that the rest of the hospital would be under lockdown soon. "While we're on lockdown, keep the patients in group A on light sedatives."

"Okay," Ginny replied. "What about group B?"

"Keep 'em on the heavier doses until we can get some help."

"Got it."

Angela hung up the intercom and stared at the wall, overwhelmed at the thought of all the vulnerable people who were threatened by that mind-destroying entity. "I don't know what this is, but I'm going to stop it," she said quietly. "I will not lose any more of you."

Once she had finished helping the long-term-care staff and had ensured that they could carry on without her, she left that wing of the hospital and headed back to the emergency ward. The halls along the way were crowded with extra beds occupied by sedated patients. Even some of the hospital staff had succumbed to what many were calling a "mind plague." Angela returned to the emergency ward, to the nurse's station where

Ginny, looking weary, was on the phone. "Ginny, where are the consultants from Central? I thought they were supposed to be here by now."

Her friend covered the mouthpiece. "Dr. Williams says they left an hour ago. He's called the police to look for them."

"Okay. Let me know as soon as they arrive."

Whispers echoed in the hallway. Angela lifted her head, eyes wide, heart racing. The voices resolved into a chorus, speaking rhythmically but unintelligibly.

"Ginny, can you hear that?"

"Hear what?" Ginny said. Then her eyes rolled back in her head, and she launched backward in a convulsive movement, crashing into the chair and cabinets behind her to lie in a crumpled heap on the floor.

"Ginny!" Angela rushed around the counter to the nurse. As Angela approached Ginny and began to kneel by her side, she hesitated, seeing that, despite her immobile body and glazed eyes, the nurse was speaking.

"Opener... opener... open the way..." mumbled the nurse.

Angela had thought that the chorus she had heard a moment ago was a psychic phenomenon, but she realized that the chant was being repeated by voices in the physical world all around her. Angela stood slowly and turned her head. All along the corridor, the patients in extra beds were sitting up.

"Opener... opener... open the way. Let me in," they chanted in unison.

Angela backed away from Ginny, shaking her head. Then all of the patients flopped back on the beds, and silence descended. She heard a moan and turned to see Ginny clambering to her feet, clutching her side.

"What... what happened?" Ginny's face was white.

Angela helped her to her seat. "You collapsed and hit that cabinet. We need to check you out. Can you walk? I'll take you to the ER."

Ginny shook her head, color returning to her face. "No, I'll be okay. Feels like a bruise, that's all."

Angela knew she needed to confront whatever the thing was before it hurt anyone else. She decided to try dream-walking again, this time with a sleeping patient. She hoped that whatever barrier she had encountered with Cassandra would not be there. "Okay. I've got to—I need to go. There's something I've got to do."

Angela patted Ginny on the shoulder and turned away. She went to one of the extra beds in the hallway and looked down at the patient. He was too heavily sedated and showed signs of shock. Angela did not want to risk the chance that the patient's trauma would interfere with the dream-walk, so she continued searching. She went to another bed and looked at the clipboard. The man was strong, and though he was heavily sedated, he looked as if he were lightly sleeping.

"You'll do," Angela said. She pushed the bed into a room that was already occupied by several other sedated patients, closed the door behind her, and locked it. "Okay, whatever you are. Here I come." She hesitated then placed her hand on the patient's forehead. She opened herself to the dream-walk, but she did not feel the usual sinking sensation that heralded departure. Her talent had never failed her before, and shaken to her core, Angela took a deep breath and held her hand on the man's forehead for several more minutes. Nothing happened. "God damn it," she muttered.

She walked over to one of the sedated patients and touched her on the forehead. Again, nothing happened. "What the hell is going on?"

Angela unlocked the door and left the room with its extra occupant. Her pace quickening, she went to another bed in the hallway. Without bothering to push it and its occupant into a room, she touched the woman's forehead. Nothing. She turned and looked all around at the strangely silent corridor. The overhead lights flickered, and she stiffened. The walls seemed to flex around her, and darkness descended. She yelped when she felt a crashing blow on her shoulders, and she clapped her head in both hands and moaned in pain as a heavy pressure squeezed her skull. She heard a vast, deep sound that grew louder—a sound like a rising wind—and the pressure receded. Then the scene rippled again before her horrified eyes. All of the patients on their beds appeared to have become rotting corpses, similar to what she had seen in the morgue with Roger. She glanced at the one nearest her and saw that its eyes were open. The skull was exposed with a gaping hole in it and was hollow. Angela choked in nausea and, backing away, felt herself stumble. Just as in the call room that morning, hands rose up out of the floor to grasp at her feet. Angela began kicking at them, but her frantic action only seemed to make things worse, until finally she stopped herself with an effort. Panicking would not help here.

She lowered her hands and closed her eyes. Visualizing the light that evoked her inner strength, in her mind's eye she saw her body begin to glow. When she opened her eyes, though, the darkness all around her was overwhelming. She felt a tingling in her scalp and heard a high-pitched sound that grew louder, like a screaming saw. The crush returned with renewed vigor and pain exploded behind her eyes.

"Get... out... of my... head." The effort to hold the intrusion at bay was sapping her strength, and her body trembled. The air changed around her, and she felt the breeze of the Other-world on her skin. The noise kept rising in a crescendo, and Angela fought with all of her energy. Suddenly, the pressure dissipated, as light flared beyond her closed eyelids. Angela staggered as she opened her eyes, and she avoided falling by grabbing the back of the nearest bed. She groaned as nausea wrenched her gut, and she barely made it to a utility sink before she emptied her stomach into it.

Angela rinsed out her mouth at the sink and sent the contents swirling down the drain. She had a terrible headache and knew she was experiencing the symptoms of massive dehydration such as she would feel with a hangover. What she needed was a megadose of vitamin B12, so she started searching the cabinet by the sink, drawer by drawer. Normally, the nurses organized the supplies, and she did not need to know where all of the emergency supplements were. She found a box of hypodermic needles and took one out. With a practiced hand, she swabbed her arm and performed the injection. As her head cleared, she looked around the hallway for shadows but saw none.

"Granddad!" The events of the morning had driven the thought of calling George out of her mind. Taking out her cell phone, she entered his number.

"Pick up, pick up," she muttered. "Granddad?"

Her grandfather's tone was agitated. "Angel? I've been trying to reach—"

"I know," Angela interrupted. "Something's going on here. I need to know what you were talking about. The shadow...?"

"Yes. You are dealing with a being. A spirit. It has taken over your hospital, and I cannot see through the darkness from here."

Angela leaned on the desk. "Look, I don't really believe in spirits. But I don't know who else to talk to. The whole ward is out of control. You remember Cassandra Grey, the girl who we thought died in that fire? Well, she didn't die." She swallowed, hearing him gasp on the other end of the line, then plunged on. "I've been treating her as her chovihani. It was going so well. But now she's in a coma, and whatever she was experiencing has spread."

"I will come to you," George said. "Wait for me."

"Wait! I—" But Angela was too late, and she heard the dial tone. "Dammit!" What she wanted was information, but now she would have to worry about her grandfather.

As she hung up, the air filled with speech and clattering equipment. For a moment she thought it was another attack, and she shrank away from the crowd of men who rushed into the corridors. Then she realized that the police had arrived.

George drove his ancient, dusty Cadillac toward the hospital. He was singing in the Romani tongue and keeping a sharp, vigilant eye on the road. He had dropped into a deep trance in order to find the quickest route, and though his driving seemed sloppy, he avoided obstacles and traffic with ease.

The hospital loomed ahead and to the right. His eyes were off the road for only a moment, but then he had to slam on the brakes to avoid colliding with a car that had pulled out of a side street in front of him. He drove slowly around it, noticing that the driver watched him with a blank stare. Then, as he approached an intersection, a panel truck ran the stoplight to block his path. He swerved, barely avoiding it.

"*Kuraf'te mulo kokalo!*" he swore. Soon he was forced to turn left onto a one-way road because traffic had completely stopped in front of him. The next crossroad was also one-way to the left, and as he approached it, he felt a headache come on that rapidly worsened. He had to stop at the light, and as he did so, a crushing weight descended and settled in his brain. He closed his eyes, gritted his teeth, and pushed back against the overwhelmingly invasive sensation. A droning voice drifted into and out of his hearing, and he saw flashing lights behind his eyelids. An eternity later, the pressure disappeared and he felt a wave of nausea. Ignoring the impatient honking of horns behind him, George opened the door, leaned out, and vomited. He wiped his mouth and swore again. Closing the car door, he accelerated through the intersection. Whatever had tried to enter his mind had failed, but he was willing to bet that it had succeeded for many of the people in the area, as evidenced by the numerous blockades he had to evade. If the Soul Thief had that kind of power outside the hospital, he shuddered to think of what it could do in its conquered territory.

As he drove, he found that every time he tried to turn right toward the hospital, another obstacle presented itself. In every case, the people involved stared blankly at him. After one particularly grueling escape, he saw a police cruiser in his rearview mirror with its lights on. Muttering angrily, he pulled over. The policeman took his time getting out of the patrol car, and George rolled down his window with his driver's license in his hand as the man stepped up to the side of his car. The policeman said nothing but simply stood by the window, staring into the car.

Losing patience, George said, "So are you going to tell me what I did wrong?"

"Do you know what you did wrong?" replied the officer in a dull monotone.

George scowled. "I was driving under the speed limit. I did not run any lights—"

The officer interrupted. "I'll tell you what you did wrong." He leaned on the car door and looked blankly at George. "You tried to go to her rescue."

George stared in shock for a moment. Then he started the car, slammed it into gear, and took off. As he sped away, he saw the policeman in the rearview mirror, watching but not moving to go after him.

"*Du te dracu!*"

It seemed to George as if he were driving an obstacle course, as pedestrian after pedestrian jumped in his path. Finally, George slammed on the brakes at a stoplight and leaned his head on the steering wheel.

"Oh Angel." He nearly sobbed. He pounded his fist on the dashboard and lifted his head to stare angrily at the hospital roof, which loomed higher than all the other buildings. He knew that if he tried to continue on foot he would be pulled down by a crowd of mind-controlled pedestrians, and he suspected that his invisibility trick, already proven useless while he was driving, would not help him avoid them. His knowledge having failed him, he knew that he needed help. The only person whose knowledge equaled or exceeded his was Nadia, his sister, who had declared Angela and him marimé years ago, but he was damned if he would let Roma custom endanger his granddaughter. He pulled into the intersection and turned left, away from the hospital and toward where Nadia lived.

"My sister will help us. I will not give up on you, Granddaughter."

The extra beds were wheeled away as, one by one, some of the less critical patients were transferred by ambulance to San Francisco Central. The hospital doors had been locked and were guarded by a detachment of policemen, and several hospital police were assisting the security contractors and city cops with the lockdown.

The security chief, a muscular, balding man whom everyone at the hospital called Big John, approached Angela.

"Dr. Lindquist has called a meeting in the second-floor conference room."

"Thanks, John. Listen, have you seen an elderly, white-haired man with a huge beard? I've been waiting for him. His name's George."

He consulted a notepad. "No. No one by that name."

"If you do, please page me."

John nodded and went back to assisting the police. Angela made her way through the bustle and reached an elevator. An orderly was guiding an empty bed onto the elevator, so rather than try to squeeze on board, Angela detoured to the stairs and climbed.

The second-floor corridor was crowded with administrative staff and security officers. As she neared the conference room, Angela saw a group of doctors and nurses gathered outside it. The door opened, and they entered, the last one holding it open for her.

The large table in the room was crowded, and everyone looked exhausted. A whiteboard, incongruously hanging under the elaborate moldings decorating the wall, had been set up at one end. Dr. Lindquist was at the head of the table, energetic and alert. He beamed. "Dr. Cooper! Welcome. Please take a seat. We're about to start."

Angela found a chair and sat. The room was silent as Josef took a moment to aim his ebullient smile at everyone in the room.

"We've had a trying time at the hospital lately. I want you to know that I appreciate all your hard work. Particularly yours, Dr. Cooper."

He paused. No one applauded. Josef shrugged, unfazed by their lack of enthusiasm. "I have good news. We are getting some temporary staff from Central. They've assigned psychiatrists and interns to our emergency ward to help with the increased workload."

The news was received with sincere applause, as well as

several exclamations of "Great!" and "About time!"

"Finally, we will soon be hiring more permanent doctors and nurses. The grant came through."

There was more applause.

"Now, as you know, the hospital is on lockdown." Josef waved a comical finger in admonition. "No one knows yet what caused the outbreak of psychoses, but we're doing what we can. I'm sure everything will be better soon." He turned away, his hands clasped behind his back. The others watched him uncertainly. Then he turned back to face Angela.

"Let's proceed with departmental reports, starting with the new rTMS trial. Dr. Cooper, how is it going?"

"The trial is going well. But this outbreak is extremely troubling—"

Josef interrupted. "I don't think the two are related, do you?" He laughed. "I understand you've had at least one success so far."

"I wouldn't call it a success. More like a failure," Angela said. "Patient C has succumbed to complete neurological collapse. She's almost completely non-responsive."

Several of the others frowned at that news, but Josef kept smiling. "Good, good. Dr. Richards, can you give a summary of what your department's doing?"

Angela's mind spun. Had Josef lost his mind? It was bad news for the trial, but he reacted as if she had told him he had won the lottery. She was speechless. One of the doctors stood and spoke.

"We're managing..." he began. His words blurred into a background drone, and the room took on a dreamlike quality.

Angela found herself staring at Dr. Lindquist. Though he was not looking at her, she had the distinct impression that he was aware of her gaze. Then, to her mounting horror, the room darkened and filled with whispers.

When the sound dispersed and the room lightened again, a new voice was speaking. That time, it was Josef. "Let's get back to it, then."

Angela realized she had missed everything that Richards and the other department heads had said, as well as much of Josef's speech. "We'll meet again tomorrow at the same time. Thanks, everyone."

The staffers stood up and shambled out of the room. Angela wanted to talk to Josef to learn why he was behaving so uncharacteristically, but she knew she had a lot of work ahead of her with the lockdown. As she prepared to leave, Josef cleared his throat. "Dr. Cooper, can you stay for a moment? I have something I need to go over with you."

Angela sighed, and Josef beckoned her. She walked over to where he was standing by his chair.

"You're one of our best staff psychiatrists. You've proven your strength to me." Josef stared at Angela and stopped smiling. "I need your gift, my Angel."

Shocked, Angela tried to back away from him, but she was not quick enough. Josef clasped her cheeks in his hands, and everything else in the room blurred, though his face took on greater clarity. She could make no sound, but there was a scream of tension in her mind. Her soul light grew again as Josef's face changed. It became darker and inhumanly beautiful. It changed into the faces of Cassandra and then Roger. There was a brilliant flash, and he receded and vanished. A dull roar filled Angela's ears, giving way to a deep hum, and then nothing.

George's car skidded to a stop in front of a gaily decorated mobile home in south San Francisco. It was located in a seedy trailer park and, like his boat, resembled the traditional *vardo* of the Roma with its elaborate carved fretwork and painted wooden trim. Ignoring the protest of his creaking bones, George leaped out and hurried toward the door. It opened as he approached, revealing a stout figure, her arms crossed.

"Nadia! I need you." George puffed with exertion.

"Georgie, I saw her in a vision, a vision full of shadows. It's Angela, isn't it?"

George moved as if to go into the house, but Nadia barred his way. "George, you know I cannot speak to you. You have been declared unclean by the clans."

George gave her an anguished look. "The shadow that killed the Greys has come back, and it will kill Angela. You saw my Angel? Then you know this is true." He reached one hand toward his sister, palm up. A succession of emotions crossed her face—anger, pity, wounded pride, and something George had never seen before: fear. His fate and that of his granddaughter were caught in the balance of that woman's power in the community, and she was afraid.

"This shadow devours souls. It is a Soul Thief, and it will take one of our own." His tone deepened with the strength of his feelings. "Can this creature, this son of Beng, be allowed its freedom because we will not change?"

Nadia lowered her arms to her sides, and her eyes filled with tears. "Oh Georgie."

She stepped aside, and he squeezed past her, into the trailer. She closed the door and hobbled to her overstuffed chair, lowering herself carefully into it. George started pacing.

"Stop pacing," Nadia snapped. "I can't concentrate when you do that."

George stopped and looked at her helplessly. "I cannot find my Angel. I tried to go to the hospital, but the Soul Thief has taken the minds of the people all around and made them into guardians. They blocked me."

"Tell me about this Soul Thief." Nadia's composure had returned. So George filled her in on his own research, including his attempted evocations of aid from the spirit world.

Nadia nodded. "We have no lore to tell us about this creature, about its weaknesses or its powers. We must tread carefully. It has a power that this world has not seen for many, many years." She paused. "Georgie, I will look for her. Make us some tea."

George went to the kitchenette and started a kettle of water boiling. Rummaging through the tea drawer, he said, "She called me from the hospital. I think the Soul Thief has taken over the place."

"There's a lot of good food for it there. Crazy people, sad people, angry people."

George dropped tea bags into a couple of mugs. "And Angela. It wants her soul, I know it."

"If it gets her soul, it gets her gift. You're right; we must hurry. Come here and kneel next to me."

George went to her side and dropped down to his knees a bit clumsily. Nadia placed her hands on his head.

"You are the strongest link to Angela. Be silent so I may see."

Quiet descended. The sound of traffic filtered through the thin walls. Then a faint keening started as the kettle of water boiled, but neither Nadia nor George went to take it off the burner. Soon it was screaming. Nadia's eyes were rolled back in her head while George swayed in place on his knees.

Suddenly Nadia cried out. Her eyes opened wide, and she seemed to be staring into another world.

"Not for you... Look to your past... Find yourself." She groaned and started to sway as well. "He is... He is... The dark one rises, shadow long, he takes the angel's healing song!"

A wind briefly rattled the trailer, and the kettle shrieked. Nadia continued her chant. "A cast-off shell in mortal hell, she wanders lost in sleeping spell!"

George opened tear-filled eyes. "But where, Nadia? Where?"

Nadia did not acknowledge him but continued in a singsong. "Seek her there where no one cares, a tender loin in darkness bare." Nadia opened her eyes and shuddered, blinking.

"I see her now," George said. In his mind, an image formed of Angela as she crouched, shivering, somewhere in the city. He felt a gentle pull on his thoughts and knew he could follow it to her.

"Georgie! You must hurry. She is in mortal danger." Nadia's voice rose with urgency. George staggered to his feet and turned to leave. "But please take that kettle off," Nadia added.

He lurched into the kitchen and turned off the fire. Then, his legs having recovered from the kneeling position, he hurried on surer feet to the door. He stopped for a moment, looking back at Nadia. "Sister, thank you. We will come back here. I think we will need you again soon."

He flung the door open and hurried out.

Angela drifted timelessly in an infinite well of darkness, a bodiless awareness with no sense of self. Then a voice whispered her name, and in a rush, her body's weight returned along with a deep gasp of breath and a leaping heartbeat. She was sprawled on the ground in absolute blackness. She was unable to see anything, not even her own hand as she held it in front of her face, and her breath was loud in the silence. She eased herself to her feet and groped carefully. She touched a rough texture, and then a stabbing pain raked her fingers, making her hiss as she jerked her hand back. As her eyes gradually adjusted, she saw that she was in the midst of the Otherworld forest, whose trees pressed close all around her. She had no idea how Josef, or whoever the spirit was, had been able to push her to that place, but she was afraid that he was in control, and she felt a lump of panic in her throat.

She inched her way from tree to tree, occasionally tangling her feet in the undergrowth. She told herself to keep moving. Perhaps she could avoid discovery if she ventured farther from where she arrived.

Moments later, she came to the edge of the forest. She hoped that she had escaped back to her own clearing. It was at least a chance to be free of confinement while she took stock of her surroundings. Perhaps she could find a path that would take her back to the physical world. She stepped forward cautiously.

"Where am I?"

The woman in the hospital waiting room stiffened in her chair. "Where am I?" she said in a toneless voice. Then she groaned and held her head.

Without warning, Angela was blinded by daylight. She shielded her eyes, waiting for them to adjust, hoping that she was indeed in home territory. When she was able to survey the clearing, she felt despair. It was not her own place, for it was cluttered with dense shrubbery and overgrown from neglect. Whoever was associated with the clearing did not spend much time in introspection. Angela had never before been able to enter the consciousness of another person without a physical touch, so she had no idea how that would affect her experience of the place or how she would be able to find her way out.

She walked carefully toward the center of the meadow, which mounded into a small hill. Perhaps a path could be found there. She wondered what would happen if she did find a way back to the physical world. Would she find herself back in the hospital? Or would she, as she suspected, reappear near the person to whom the field belonged?

As she moved, a breeze arose, lightly at first, but as she neared the hill, it whipped into a gale that pushed her to her knees. Something did not want her there. She turned and crawled away from the hill, and the wind rapidly diminished in force. Then she heard a low chuckling.

"Did you think you could escape me?" said the familiar voice.

"You can't escape me," said the woman.

"Miss, are you okay?" asked the registration clerk.

The woman just moaned in pain.

Angela turned and ran back toward the woods. As she entered, the daylight vanished abruptly, and she collided with a tree. She began stumbling through dense undergrowth, hands outstretched, fending off more collisions, and her breath quickened and echoed in her ears as if she were in an enclosed space. After a moment, she fell to her knees. The brush had given way once again, and visible against a vast, starry night sky were the dim shapes of the trees all around. However, at the moment she could not tell whether it was a path or a full clearing.

Angela stood and resumed her tentative walk. There was a dim glow to her right, so she turned in that direction and approached it. As she neared it, the glow resolved into a strange, flame-like shape, visible among the trunks of trees and twisted creepers. It appeared to be a campfire of a sort, but the flames were motionless and silvery. Seated to the side of the "fire" was a dark, hunched figure, making faint, muttering sounds that resolved into words. "Lost, all lost. Where are you, girl? Let's find her."

The words stopped, and the figure reached up to lower the cowl of its robe, revealing an ancient, wizened face crowned with white hair. "Don't be afraid," said a quavering voice. "Come sit by me and warm your bones."

Angela hesitated, but she felt no sense of threat from the stranger. She sat on her haunches, close enough to be illuminated by the "flames" but ready to run if need be. "Who are you?"

"Me? I'm nobody special. You, on the other hand, are very special indeed."

"What? Why?"

"Your time is running out, dear. Listen closely. I have something important to tell you."

The figure leaned closer to the campfire, and Angela saw that it was a very old woman. Her eyes were white with cataracts, but she nevertheless looked directly at Angela. "You must look to your past to find your future. Go deeper into the Wood. Find your true self, your ancient and ever-present self." She turned her head furtively as if she had heard a sound. Then her sightless eyes returned to Angela. "Now go!"

The old woman raised her hands as if to shoo Angela away, and she and her fire receded rapidly into the distance. Soon Angela was alone in the clearing. She rose to walk, and as she took a step toward the edge of the clearing, she was blinded by a burst of light and raised her hands protectively over her face.

Angela waited until her eyes had recovered from being dazzled before taking her hands away. She saw that she was standing in a desolate, blasted place with no sign of the forest. The sky above was orange, streaked with dust, while the earth below was barren, rocky ground in all directions. Standing directly in front of her was a space-suited figure. The person was looking the other way, and Angela froze in fear.

A thin wind tugged at the protective gear. There was gray ash swirling in the air, partially obscuring the valley below. Angela heard unintelligible words coming from the person. They were in no language that she had ever heard. Then Angela shook her head as a buzzing filled her ears. The buzzing resolved itself into English speech that echoed oddly.

"No more. We're leaving you in peace." The voice was high in tone, feminine. Then the figure stiffened and raised its arms. In a curious singsong, the figure intoned: "When twenty thousand turns of the world about the sun have passed, I shall return to the world of flesh. Then you and I shall contend once again."

The figure lowered its arms and kicked at the ground, raising a puff of fine, ashy dust that blew away in the thin wind. Then, it turned toward Angela. Through the glass faceplate, Angela could see that it was a woman's face that closely resembled her own but with more angular features. The woman did not appear to see her, though, as she walked with a determined stride toward and past Angela. Angela turned to watch and gasped as she saw her waver and vanish like a heat mirage.

The wind howled and blew the entire scene away, leaving Angela standing in a forest clearing. A vast shadow, hovering above, descended abruptly and, swirling like a small tornado, condensed into human shape. Standing directly in front of Angela was a darkly dressed man who strongly resembled Josef Lindquist.

Angela yelled and then backed away. The man smiled, then

his form exploded, fragmenting into a sense-bewildering storm of colors and shapes, while the air was filled with a cacophony of sounds. As she turned to run into the forest, she glanced over her shoulder. The man had coalesced again and was hovering directly behind her, staying with her as she ran. She tripped and fell, flipped herself over to face him, and scrabbled backward, raising her hands to ward off an expected blow.

The man laughed. "Angel. Forgive my appearance. The stitching on all these souls doesn't seem to be holding." His voice changed gender and inflection while his form continued to shift and blur. Angela glimpsed faces that she recognized, including Roger's and the faces of others from the hospital.

"Back off! I don't know what you are, but you will not take me," she shouted.

The man opened his arms in a peaceable gesture then clasped his hands together. "Angel, I already have you. I've had you since you got here. You were too strong on earth for me, but here, in my home territory, I am the master." He snorted with scorn. "You don't remember me, do you? You don't even know who you just saw. That woman was you. You kept me trapped here in this dream world while the others escaped to earth, so long ago. I've been looking for you since your rebirth. And now..."

The man raised both arms toward Angela and spread his fingers. Her mind was consumed by a blaze of agony that burned away all sense of her body. Then the pain disappeared abruptly as the world blurred into blobs of light. She felt a pulling sensation where the pit of her stomach would be as the light intensified. She heard a strange hiss from the man's direction, her heart clenched, and the light went away abruptly.

Angela sobbed and felt a cold breeze on her body. As she regained her senses, she realized that she was naked and crouching, overwhelmed by a sense of defeat. A golden glow briefly occluded her vision, and she wept as a force drew something precious from a most private place within. She looked up and cringed to see that the man's form had grown.

The Soul Thief sighed. "What a lovely gift you have brought me. I shall treasure it. And now I believe we are to be wed once again, beloved."

"She is not for you, old man," snapped an angry voice. Startled, Angela turned her head to see the old woman from the campfire standing by her side. "Or do you want her to finish the job she started so long ago?"

"Do not come between me and my prey," he snarled.

"She is no prey of yours," said the woman in warm tones. "And neither am I."

The old woman shifted in shape, revealing herself as Angela's great-aunt Nadia, her grandfather's sister. Angela crawled away while the Soul Thief was distracted. Something caught her eye: a spot of pavement on the forest floor. She sprang toward it, and the howl of outrage from the Soul Thief dwindled as Angela collapsed into darkness.

10.

SHERI SAT at the street corner as she always did on Wednesdays, her possessions arrayed in plastic bags behind her, and a large sign on the sidewalk beside her proclaimed that she would work for money. She had just eaten at the soup kitchen, and being well wrapped against the chilly June night, she was in a good mood. Several tourists had already thrown coins in the soup can that she held out as they passed, and one gentleman, a very nice gentleman at that, had put a ten-dollar bill in it.

Allowing the street sounds to wash over and through her, it took her a few minutes to notice that something was amiss. Several pedestrians across the street had doubled over, clutching their heads and groaning. To her disgust, she noticed that one had thrown up on the sidewalk, and she decided that a party must have let out somewhere. Then she heard a cacophony of horns and a shattering crash of glass and saw that someone had rear-ended a car in the street directly in front of her. Expecting to see angry motorists clambering out of their cars, she was surprised that both were leaning out of their open driver's-side doors and vomiting onto the pavement. Then it seemed as if the entire scene froze, as almost all the pedestrians on the block stopped and clutched their heads. The air was filled with their cries of pain, and Sheri lumbered to her feet, ready to run from whatever was causing the commotion.

"You will find her," shouted one of the men nearby, as he straightened from his earlier, agony-induced bend. Sheri flinched.

"Find my beloved..." Sheri jumped as another man behind her shouted. Then she shrieked when she felt a hand grab her arm roughly, and she yanked herself free of the grasp of a man who had approached her unnoticed. She was now staring at a ring of faces, all of which looked drunk or stoned. She half crouched, preparing to rush one of them and escape, when the tall black man in front of her spoke.

"Submit to the master," he said in a deep, calm voice. "Why do you resist?"

"I don't know nuthin'. Get away from me!"

Without warning, her head exploded with agony. A flaring light filled her vision as she screamed and doubled over. A hammering, insistent command thundered in her skull. "Find my beloved and bring her to me." She had enough time to wonder who the "beloved" was, and then she knew no more.

Night in the Tenderloin was alive with traffic and voices. The city park, deserted, was closed for the night. Leaning against a fence that surrounded a basketball court near the center of the park, Angela huddled, naked and shivering. She shook violently and clung to the fence to avoid falling. She moaned and stumbled away, aching in every part of her body. She barked her shin on a bench, reached out to grasp it, collapsed onto it, and curled up, making no effort to cover herself, as her consciousness guttered out.

Awakening from dreams of pursuit, Angela was still curled up on the bench. The watery light of early dawn was accompanied by the sounds of more cars but fewer voices. She stirred, arose, and looked around. The world was surreal and shifting and seemed full of phantoms. Her breath was rapid and loud in her own ears, and all other sounds were muffled. Otherworldly shadows crowded her peripheral vision, and she could not focus on anything. She was little more than a bundle of instincts and raw nerves.

She hugged her arms to herself and walked slowly to the fence surrounding the park. She stood in place while vehicles and pedestrians passed in front of her, until several people noticed her. One woman gasped, exclaimed, and hurried off while several teenagers pointed and laughed. A man talking on his cell phone saw her; his eyes widened, and he hurried away. The sounds those people made were surreal and distant. After a time, the gawkers lost interest. Other passersby turned to look at her, but they registered no surprise, simply blank indifference. The roar of traffic died down, and the pedestrians all stopped walking. Those nearest her turned to face her and spoke in unison. "You are mine. You will never escape me."

A wave of fright made Angela shrink back and crouch, shivering in the chill morning air. She felt a deep part of herself rise up in defense and saw her surroundings begin to crowd with shadows. She ran on trembling legs back into the park, caught herself against a light post, and glanced back, only to see that the pedestrians were once again indifferent to her.

The effort of running left her gasping for breath, and all she could hear were her own lungs that sounded like monstrous bellows. Her vision swam, and she was barely able to keep her balance as she continued walking. Soon she approached the other side of the small park. Reaching out, she clutched the fence with both hands. At that moment, she heard a rattling of chain and padlock, and she turned to see a park attendant unlocking the gate giving access to the park. He did not appear to notice her standing nearby, but a sense of self-consciousness made her cover herself with one hand as the man opened the gate.

After he left, Angela cautiously approached the exit and proceeded aimlessly down Eddy Street. She ducked from entryway to entryway in the not-yet-open businesses lining the street.

The city continued to appear surreal and shadowy. Time itself seemed unstable. The few pedestrians she saw at first walked at half the normal pace, and then they accelerated until they were walking twice as fast as normal. The otherworldly impressions coalesced into faces and forms and brief snatches of imagery from recent days. Angela collapsed in terror as the desolate wasteland replaced the waking world completely, and the smiling Soul Thief stood before her, mocking her. Then her vision of the street returned, and after a moment, she drew herself back up from her half-sprawling position.

The day continued to brighten. A flash caught her eye, and she stopped walking to hide behind a garbage receptacle as she saw a police squad car turn down the street, its lights on. Faintly, she heard the whoop of the siren, but as soon as the car was halfway down the block, it slowed and then stopped at an angle that blocked further traffic. The policeman stepped out, looked incuriously in Angela's direction, and hurried away, abandoning the car.

As Angela hid, she saw the shadows created by her invisibility charm begin to dissipate, draining away as exhaustion overwhelmed her. Angela crept over to a wall and collapsed against it, sitting propped up and hunched over.

She flinched when a piping voice asked, "Lady, are you all right?" Angela looked up blearily, barely able to acknowledge the young boy who was standing in front of her on the sidewalk. Two adults approached, evidently the child's parents, and all three stared at Angela impassively.

"Return to me," they said in unison. "Join me, my beloved."

She cowered away from them, raising her hands in an attempt to ward them off. As the boy came closer, his finger outstretched, she turned her face away. Then she heard a muffled thud, and when she looked back, she saw that all three were collapsed on the pavement, twitching and thrashing. They stopped moving and lay still. Other pedestrians walked around them without noticing. Then Angela heard a weirdly modulated screech, like car tires but distorted. There was a slam, and a brilliantly lit human figure strode toward her, scattering the shadows. A wave of sound pushed forward as pedestrians broke into concerned babble. Angela lifted her head and squinted into the light.

"Granddad?" she croaked.

She tried to rise but was still weak. She moaned.

"Good God. Angel!"

Boots clattered, and then an arm encircled her waist, and her own left arm was lifted over strong shoulders. As she was pulled up, she managed to place her feet on the ground. George helped her stagger over to his car, which was outlined vividly in front of her with more of the strange, bright light. With his help, Angela half fell into the passenger side of the car, and after the door shut behind her, she heard the driver's side open. As the car smoothly accelerated, Angela's consciousness slipped.

George pulled into a tow-away zone two blocks away from where he had found Angela, hoping that the strangely affected people would no longer be a threat there. He parked and reached over to coax her into a more upright position. He lifted her chin and peered at her half-closed eyes. "Angel! Angela. Can you hear me?"

With his other hand, he picked up his water bottle and dribbled some liquid onto her mouth, which looked cracked and raw. She licked her lips and parted them, so he squirted a little more in. She swallowed and opened her bloodshot eyes.

"Granddaughter, it's me. I found you. What happened to you?"

He looked at her injuries, incredulous. Angela looked as if she had been in a car accident. He stripped off his windbreaker and used it to cover her. "We must get you to the hospital. Not Franklin."

Angela stirred weakly and pushed him away with her hands. "No... No, no," she groaned, and coughs shook her body.

"Why? Never mind, you're right. That thing might be at Central Hospital, too."

He looked at her again and opened his inner sight. "O *Del!* Angel. What has that thing done to your soul?" There was a shadow that clung to her in tatters, giving her the appearance of a decaying corpse in his second sight. Galvanized by the new horror, he pulled back into the relatively deserted street. "We will go to my boat. It is closer than Nadia's place, and my tools are there." They proceeded toward the marina.

As he drove, he gestured at the street. "Something has happened to the people. When I got closer to you, it looked like they had lost their souls. All of them were empty. Not like the guardians who stopped me before." He looked around. "Now they look normal. It is as if you were at the center of a storm. It was that demon. That spirit. I think it is seeking you and cannot find you."

He glanced at Angela and saw that she had fallen asleep. George continued driving, muttering anxiously.

George's car pulled into a parking spot. The marina was peaceful, and the sailboat masts near where he parked swayed gently to an inshore breeze. George got out of the car and leaned back in through the passenger side window. "Angela, wait here. I will get some clothes."

He hesitated, his fear for her sickening in its intensity. She was so crumpled and blank, nearly vanishing in the folds of his windbreaker. Finally, he shut the door, locked it, and walked rapidly toward the security gate for his pier.

For what seemed like an eternity, Angela remained huddled in the seat, unable to think, staring at the scene around her as her own breathing and rapping heartbeat filled her ears. Once she heard what sounded like a strange human scream, but after her heart stopped racing, she saw that it was one of the seagulls that thronged the air above the piers.

Through the windshield, she saw George return, first moving slowly then faster. Everything blurred again, and when the car door slammed, the sound was muted. When George spoke, his words were unintelligible.

"Put this on. Can you hear me, Angel?" George sighed and helped his granddaughter struggle into a pair of sweatpants and an oversized shirt. He slipped a pair of flip-flops on her feet and half carried her out of the car. She was unsteady but seemed to be able to walk with assistance.

George led her cautiously, pausing to open the security gate and maneuver her through it. They made their way along the pier. Someone on a neighboring boat waved at George. "Hey, George! Is that Angela? Is she okay?"

George waved back. "She is fine. Hangover!"

The vacationer laughed. George kept walking with Angela toward his boat.

Angela heard the laughter of the vacationer, which sounded like a hyena's bark. Ahead, one of the boats appeared to be sharper in appearance than the others, almost glowing with reality, and on the prow, the name "Gypsy Angel" scintillated in the morning sun. Her breath quickened, and George made an exclamation. Angela could understand what he said. "Angel! Slow down. You might fall."

Angela felt her body move of its own volition, dragging George to his boat. She stuck a foot out, and the world spun for a moment, but George held her firmly and kept her from falling in the water.

"Over here. Step here." He spoke in a deep bass tone.

A gangway led to a gap in the sailboat's railing, and George helped her climb aboard. The elaborately painted trim and gleaming surfaces almost made her cry with relief at the end of her shadow-haunted journey.

George helped her down the stairs and into the salon. The embroidered curtains had been drawn back from the portholes and the morning light shone on the polished teak and brass. He reached over to close a few of the curtains then swept the settee clear of books and papers. He helped Angela to sit and went to fetch water from the galley sink.

"Angel, I should not say I warned you. But I warned you. *Mi duvvaleska!*" He shook his head and came back with the water glass. Supporting her shoulders, he held it to her mouth. She took the water mechanically, but the stunned, half-asleep look never left her face.

"You are gone, yes," he muttered. "I will fetch your *lesko thi*, your soul."

He set the glass down, and after making sure she was comfortable, he disappeared down the passageway. "It has been too long since I have retrieved a soul." Rummaging through the wooden chest at the foot of the master berth, he began pulling out colorful cloth and embroidered bags. Quickly removing his shirt, he pulled on the costume of the Rom shaman, the tribal chovihano. He dragged a series of necklaces and talismans out of a box in the chest, solemnly donned them, and finished by tying a kerchief on his head. Picking up a smaller box from the chest, he hurried back to the dining salon and set the small box down on the table.

Lowering Angela to a prone position, George adjusted her legs, crossed her arms on her belly, and covered her with a small blanket. He opened the box, picked up an embroidered bag, opened it, and sprinkled dust on Angela's prone figure. The words of the chant of power rolled off of his tongue as he worked. Setting the bag down, he kneeled by her side and placed his hands on her crossed arms. Closing his eyes, he began the chant that would loosen his spirit and give it mobility in the unseen world. Though he lacked Angela's unique vision and her ability to bodily enter the Otherworld, with his mind he could navigate a layer of that complex realm where the spirits lived and worked their will upon the earth. He had no idea how long it would take, but he was prepared to work as long as necessary to find and retrieve his granddaughter's soul.

Night had fallen. A half-empty glass of water was on the table near George. He was kneeling by Angela, one hand on her brow and one on top of her two hands, which were clasped on her belly. His head was down so that his arms were outstretched, and he was murmuring his chants. He took a sudden breath, and his body jerked as if electrified.

While the world continued to be dreamlike for Angela, the colors were sharper and time regained its regular flow. Sounds were more precise, and faint music overlaid everything, cutting in and out. It seemed to be emanating from George, who was shouting words of power in a strange language, words that echoed as if spoken in a vast cavern. The powder he had sprinkled sparked with light, looking almost as if it were on fire as it lay in drifts on her body.

Angela flinched when she saw a vivid vision of the wasteland flash into being and then recede. The boat returned to reality around her, but in another moment, the wasteland appeared again. It started flashing more rapidly, until finally Angela found herself standing and facing the rising sun. She felt George's hands on her shoulders as he stood behind her. She looked down at one of his hands and was not surprised to see six fingers.

"Come forth, enemy," George boomed loudly. "You stole what was not yours to take."

There was no response save for the whistling of the wind.

George continued. "By my power in this world, I compel you to give up the soul of light."

There was no response. George raised his right hand straight up, clenched his fist, and yanked down as if on an invisible cord. Thunder clapped deafeningly, and the air burst with light. The landscape swirled with a dust storm. Congealing out of the storm was a strange blob about a hundred feet away. While most of the dust disappeared, the blob remained, undulating menacingly.

"By my art, I have called you into a visible form," George said in a more conversational tone. "My enemy, give up the soul of this woman to me."

The dust spun, and a scene from the past, showing Cassandra's family burning alive, played in it briefly like a movie. George's face became sterner. "You cannot shame me, spirit. My will is greater than yours."

The earth shook, and a crack zigzagged from below the entity with lightning speed, splitting the earth below George and Angela's feet. They staggered, both falling, but George prevented Angela from sprawling as he dropped to his knees in front of her. Quickly, he plunged his arm into the crack and hauled. His arm trembled, muscles standing out in cords. His face broke into sweat. "Give... it... up," he growled through clenched teeth.

The blob was thrashing, and a pale light began streaming from out of the cracked earth. George fell back, and Angela was bathed in a pearlescent glow. A howl of rage filled the air, and the dust swirled, obscuring everything.

Early the next morning, Angela was lying on the settee. George was sprawled on the floor nearby, breathing heavily and drenched in sweat. He pushed up on one elbow.

"Angel?" he said weakly.

Angela stirred then awakened as if from deep sleep. "Grand-dad?"

"Angela! *Bad inderi!*" He staggered upright, went to Angela's side, and helped her stand, though he seemed on the verge of collapse himself.

"How did I get here?" Angela looked around at the boat. Then her face took on an alarmed expression. "Cassie! God, that thing has taken over the hospital." She staggered and fell back on the settee. "Oooooh."

George went to the galley, poured some water into a coffee cup, and brought it to her. "Here is water. Don't get up, Angel."

Angela propped herself on an elbow and sipped from the

cup, dribbling water down her chin. George's throat was parched, so he poured himself a cup of water as well and sat down next to Angela. "I found you on Eddy Street. In the Tenderloin."

Angela shook her head. "How... how did I get so far?"

"I do not know. Nadia told me where to find you." He grasped her shoulders. "The Soul Thief took you, Angel. I thought I lost you." His voice cracked on the last sentence. George brushed Angela's hair out of her face. "I found part of your soul, but I do not have your gift and I could not stand against the Soul Thief. Angel, I could not bring back your dream-walking, your specialness. He has that now." He sipped some water and coughed. "It must be why he is called the Soul Thief. He steals the best of us and takes it for himself."

Angela shuddered, her eyes fluttering. "Cassandra... She was a telepath. Now it's got her gift and mine." Angela's head lolled, and her eyes closed as she slipped into unconsciousness.

George sat for a moment longer then rose unsteadily. He looked hopelessly down at Angela. "How am I going to pick you up? You are no longer a girl." He scratched his beard and thought for a moment. "We must go to my sister. I can do no more by myself." Then he bent to haul her up into his arms and staggered to the companionway.

George pulled up to Nadia's trailer in a shower of gravel. The door slammed open, and his brother Michael, who resembled a bald and mustachioed version of himself, hurried out to the car. George got out and went around to the passenger side, and Michael helped him carry Angela's unconscious form into the trailer.

"Georgie, put her on the couch. I want to keep an eye on her," said Nadia from her chair.

They laid Angela on the couch, and Michael went to the bedroom to retrieve blankets.

"You saw me coming," George stated.

"Of course. I know you were doing a soul working for her, but I could not see what it was."

Michael came back with an armload of blankets and a pillow. He stood over Angela, face creased with concern. "She looks like she hasn't slept in weeks."

They covered her and arranged her pillow. Then George pulled up a chair from the dining room to sit close by Angela's side while Michael took his seat near Nadia.

Nadia sighed. "So is she going to live? Please tell me!"

George startled. "Good God, Nadia, I am sorry. I am almost asleep on my feet."

Nadia shook her head. George continued. "She will live. I retrieved a large part of her soul. But..." He sighed heavily. "I could not bring back her gift. She is lost without it."

Nadia groaned. "This is terrible news. It would almost have been better if she had not lived."

George glared at Nadia. "You cannot mean that! This is Angela we are discussing, not some rival sorcerer."

Nadia raised a placating hand. "I'm sorry. We're under a lot of stress here. George, that thing has her gift now. It can cross from the Otherworld to this one, and it can take people with it back to whatever hell it has created there."

Michael frowned. "What do you mean? How can someone take a gift like that? It is a part of her."

"That is the gift or curse of the Soul Thief," Nadia said, her face austere with tension. "Every soul it steals, it uses. It started with Cassandra's mother, and who knows how many others it has stolen since then."

"Is this thing a Rom ghost, a *mulo*? A curse on our people?"

George spoke up. "No, Michael. It is a curse on all mankind. Until now, it has haunted the night and has had no power to take the souls of the strong—only the weak and maddened among us. But this girl, Cassandra, she had a gift of her own, telepathy. I do not know how that gift gave the Soul Thief the power to kill and to take from the strongest of us. My Angel." His eyes welled, and a tear rolled down his weatherworn face. He wiped angrily at it.

Nadia sat quietly for a moment, thick-veined hands crossed primly in her lap, staring into space. Then she said, "It must be driven out of this world."

George stood, hands in his pockets, frowning. "With Angela's power gone, I am the only one who can confront it in its own world. Though I do not have her Sight, I know that I can face it on its own ground. When I found her soul, I was able to keep that thing from killing her."

He looked out the window. "I must go unseen to the hospital and destroy the Soul Thief. But Nadia, I could not get close to it. The guardians..."

"I know a very good invisibility trick. Go to the kitchen, and get down the jar of beans from the top shelf above the sink."

George went to the kitchen, reached above the sink, and indicated a jar. "This one?"

"Yes. It has a black circle on the label."

He noticed that the jar was nearly empty; there were two small objects that resembled pinto beans inside. He brought it back to Nadia, and she unscrewed the lid to take out a bean. "When you need to be invisible, place this under your tongue."

He shook his head. "I do not know where you learn these things."

"Never you mind." She indicated the other chairs in the room. "Both of you sit down."

George and his brother looked at her, startled, then sat slowly.

"Now, Georgie, you are not strong enough to kill that thing by yourself. It has eaten the soul of our most powerful chovihani." She raised her hand as he opened his mouth to object. "No, but I think you must go to the hospital. There is one there who has, or had, power that we can use."

George was confused. "Who...?" Then realization dawned. "Cassandra."

"Who?" Michael asked.

George turned to him. "She was Esmerelda's little girl. She survived that fire."

"O Del!" Michael sat back, shocked.

George looked back at Nadia. "I will go and rescue Cassandra and bring her back here. If I can retrieve her soul and her gift, maybe she can help us to defeat the monster."

"That is an excellent plan. Go. Bring back that poor child."

George looked at Angela's sleeping form. "What do we tell Angela? She will come to try to rescue me if she learns I have gone there."

Nadia smiled. "We will keep her here. I have made a sleeping potion. She will get all the rest she needs. Soon her strength will be needed whether or not she goes to the hospital."

George nodded and stood. "Okay. Michael, can you get some of your boys to help?"

Michael stood also. "Yes. I can get ten men. I'll tell them to guard the ways to the hospital and watch for you. I hope that is enough."

They clasped hands and hugged briefly. "I'll go, then. Wish me well."

"*Atsh me develesa*," said Michael.

George drove away fast, spinning the wheels of his Cadillac in the gravel as he departed for the hospital.

As George turned right at an intersection to drive to the hospital, he saw another car turn sharply to cut him off. He swerved, cursing. Then, remembering Nadia's gift, he took the bean out of his shirt pocket and placed it under his tongue. It tasted like dust, and he had to resist the urge to spit it out. However, as he continued driving, he noticed that there were no further obstacles. Nor did he feel the crushing weight of mental domination that had occurred the last time he had tried to approach the enemy stronghold. Nearing the hospital, he realized that the bean was slowly dissolving in his mouth, and he felt a gag reflex that he sternly resisted.

He pulled slowly into the hospital emergency entrance driveway, noticing that it looked deserted. An unnatural quiet hung over the hospital as he parked the car and killed the engine. At that moment, the bean came apart in his mouth, and he hawked and spat a spray of black mucus out his car window. He was on his own again, it seemed. He concentrated for a moment, and his surroundings became indistinct as his invisibility cloaked him. He got out of the car, shut the door quietly, and walked quickly to the entrance. Seeing no one nearby, he approached the automatic doors and, as they swooshed open, ducked inside.

No one was in the emergency foyer or at the admissions counter. He hurried to the door leading to the rest of the hospital and stopped. Standing to one side, he closed his eyes and concentrated. He visualized the girl Cassandra as a child, not knowing how she would look as a teen. But he gambled that there was still a link from that time a few years ago when the girl was caught up in what he knew now was an encounter with the Soul Thief.

An image rushed into his mind: a slim, young girl sitting in a chair, tied to it with restraints. There was a tall, laughing man with a small, neatly trimmed beard standing in front of her. The vision vanished, but George could feel a tugging in his solar plexus that guided him. He opened the door and began walking along the hallway. Soon he encountered several nurses who were helping a doctor with a patient on a gurney. He passed them unseen and continued moving through corridors that, as he neared the heart of the hospital, were thronged with busy nurses and orderlies.

Following the tug that led him one direction after another, he came to a corridor with a door at one end. A tingling sensation in his face and arms told him he was closing in on someone with power. He moved more cautiously. Flattening himself to one wall, he touched the door and extended his senses. He met a wall of resistance that occluded his inner sight, and he silently cursed. The creature had its own tricks; of that he was certain.

He gathered his strength, turned the knob, and quickly entered the room, his free hand raised and curled in a gesture of power. What he saw stopped him in his tracks. The room was far too large for the entire hospital to contain and was filled with beds that vanished into the misty distance. Standing by one of the beds near him was the laughing man of his vision. He was bent over a prone figure, touching it on the forehead. George prepared a curse while searching for a weapon.

The man dropped his hand and turned his head to look directly at George. He grinned.

George shouted a word of power and leaped forward, fists raised. There was a blinding light, and he felt a dizzying loss of balance. When George's eyesight cleared, he realized he was lying on his side on the floor. He heard chuckling, and lifting his head, he saw the man standing a few feet away, his arms crossed. George levered himself up on his elbows, his head whirling.

"I expected someone else." The man smiled indulgently. "Are you a friend of hers?"

George growled and tried getting to his feet, but he felt weak and unsteady, so he had to content himself with kneeling on one knee. "I am not important. I am here to save someone." He looked at the bed and noticed that the woman was blond, not dark haired.

The man gestured to the beds. "I'm sure you can find some-one to save here."

George wondered why he was not already dead. Clearly the man had the edge in power, yet he seemed content to talk. Deciding to prolong the conversation so he could recover his strength, George rose to a standing position and reached out to one of the beds to steady himself. "What have you done here?"

The man gestured grandly. "Here are some of my children. Or if you prefer, my descendants; I am simply... taking care of them."

George looked more closely and realized that the man's face was damp with sweat. So he, too, was struggling. Perhaps he wasn't as invulnerable as he seemed.

"I know who you are. You are the Soul Thief, the son of Beng, and you have taken the body of this man."

The man smiled. "Soul Thief. I like that. Though I don't know this 'Beng' you refer to. But I believe I know who you are now, old friend." He pointed at George, and a shadow obscured the room. The Soul Thief's smile vanished, though, and his labored breathing belied his weakness.

George snorted. "Are we friends? You stole my Angela from me. You will pay for that and for your other crimes." He scanned the beds, looking for a familiar face, but he could find no one who resembled the girl Cassandra. He took a deep breath and found that he could stand unaided.

The Soul Thief's eyes widened. "No, I think not."

George heard the door open behind him, and without hesitation, he lifted a powerful arm and swung it back as he turned, striking one of the orderlies who had come through and knocking him flat. The other orderly grabbed George from behind and attempted to put him in a shoulder lock, but George's physical strength had returned. He lifted one leg, kicked backward, and felt satisfaction as his heavy boot connected with the man's shin. Shouting in pain, the orderly fell, and George hurled himself at the Soul Thief, who retreated before his anger.

Leaping to grapple his enemy, George wrapped his powerful arms around the man and swung his considerable weight to one side and down. He dropped to the floor and landed on top of the Soul Thief, who grunted with pain. George pummeled him with powerful fists, hoping that if he could render the man unconscious, he could bind him and search for Cassandra unhindered. He delivered a right cross to the man's chin and then a glancing blow to his cheekbone while supporting himself with his left arm. The Soul Thief squirmed under his weight and brought a knee up in an attempt to push George off. George struck again but only succeeded in a grazing blow to the cheek as the man jerked his head away.

Suddenly the air became chill, and George saw darkness gathering around them as the light dimmed. Knowing that the Soul Thief was preparing a supernatural attack, George attempted to render him unconscious by grabbing his head in both hands and slamming it against the floor repeatedly but to no avail. The man's form dissolved under George, dropping him to the floor, and George's strength began to drain away. He rolled onto his back and concentrated, attempting another sorcerous attack, but a burst of light dazzled his eyes.

He felt hands grasping his jacket, and he was lifted to his

feet. When his eyes cleared, he saw that two orderlies held him securely. The Soul Thief was prone on the floor, groaning. Then George heard whispering that came from everywhere. He turned his head to try to locate the origin of the sound but could not. The sound faded.

"Bring... bring me the other vessel," said the Soul Thief weakly. "And bind him."

George struggled but was exhausted by the effort he had expended in attacking the Soul Thief. Soon he was bound to one of the empty beds with thick restraints, and he grimly held onto consciousness. One of the orderlies hurried away and came back a moment later with a dark-haired girl who had an empty expression on her face. George recognized an older version of the Cassandra that he remembered. She was completely passive, and he recognized in her the same symptoms that Angela had exhibited in the Tenderloin.

The orderly guided Cassandra to stand beside the prone Soul Thief and forced her to her knees. The Soul Thief painfully rolled to one side and lifted his hand to touch the girl's forehead. Cassandra trembled, George heard what sounded like a sob, and then she got smoothly back to her feet as the man's body fell back, unconscious. She turned to face George, and he saw in her eyes a new, malevolent awareness.

"So as you see, there is no escape from me." She laughed. "Now, what do I do with you?"

She glided over to stand over George, her face twisted in a smirk. "I want her, and I believe she will come for you, so now," she said, raising her fist, "it's time for you to sleep." She brought her fist down hard on his chest, and George felt a stab of agony. His vision tunneled, until all he saw was Cassandra's face. A roaring filled his hearing, and he knew no more.

11.

DARKNESS. THEN light. There was a roaring that gradually fell in volume, and the light resolved into blurs. As the blurs rapidly sharpened, Angela remembered herself, and wakefulness returned. She was looking at the interior of a small, crowded trailer home. Knickknacks covered shelves, while hangings and colorful art draped the walls and furniture. Then, as her bodily sensations returned in a rush, she realized that she was lying on a couch in Nadia's home, and she struggled to a sitting position. To the left of the couch, sitting in an overstuffed chair, she saw Great-Aunt Nadia watching her with a concerned look on her face. Standing by her side was her great-uncle Michael.

"Nana? Uncle Michael?" She put her hand to her face. "How did I get here? Where's Granddad?"

Michael went to her side and helped her sit up. "Shhh. Angel, you've been out awhile. Georgie left. He will be back."

"Angela, your grandfather brought you here. You were unconscious." Nadia nodded at Michael. "Get her some tea, will you?" Michael went to the kitchen. Nadia looked meaningfully at Angela. "Angela. Do you hate me for what I did?"

Angela stared at her for a moment then shook her head minutely. "What you did was nothing next to how I felt. Feel." She scrubbed her face with one hand and ran her fingers back through her impossibly knotted hair.

Nadia sighed. "What George has told me changes everything, child. It seems I owe you an apology."

Angela shuddered. "That... thing. It almost killed me. What is it?"

"Didn't Georgie tell you? It's the Soul Thief."

Angela shook her head. "Not who. What. I already know who. I share a history with that thing. It called me beloved. I have memories."

Michael made a startled grunt, and a cup rattled against its saucer. Then the kettle started screaming, and he took it off the heat to pour tea.

"I am not surprised," Nadia said. "Angela, you know I did what I did to protect our community. Your gift is not from our people. It is... old. Very old. And it can be very dangerous."

Angela sat quietly, unable to think clearly. Michael brought tea to them both and sat back down in his chair. "No one else can do what you do," he said.

"But you fought the Soul Thief," Nadia said, "and you are here, and you are alive. You still have something of yourself."

"Granddad did a soul retrieval. He risked everything for me. But he couldn't restore my... power to me."

"That's what he told me. We need to know what nature of being the Soul Thief is." Nadia sipped her tea, looking thoughtful. "The answer is to be found in your past."

Angela snapped her fingers. "You were there! I just remembered."

"What do you mean? Where?"

"You were in the Otherworld, fighting the Soul Thief. I think you saved my life there."

Nadia shook her head. "It was a struggle to see you, yes, but I don't remember encountering him. I believe that your vision of us in the Otherworld shows our oversoul, which is the highest part of us. I envy you because of that."

Angela stood up though her body trembled with exhaustion. "There's a girl, a patient of mine. She's at the hospital, and the thing took her gift too. She's in danger. They all are."

"Angela, we must know more of your memories," said Nadia. "Let me take you deep into your past."

Angela frowned and looked down. Her stomach twisted with fear and nausea, and she had to fight to keep her footing. "Nana, I'm not sure that's a good idea. I might meet him again."

"It's a risk we must take if we are to learn what we must know to defeat him. Sit back down and close your eyes."

Angela did so reluctantly.

"Let go of this time and place." Nadia's words were soothing. "Let go."

Angela heard a humming that superseded all other sound. She leaned back in the sofa as a floating sensation came over her, as if she were in a warm tub of water.

"Now tell me," Nadia continued. "Who are you?"

"Angela... Cooper." Her own voice seemed far away.

"Who are you?"

"Angela."

More forcefully, "Who are you?"

Angela breathed deeply, and a sense of vastness filled her. Her few years on the earth felt like an eyeblink against an aeon. "I am... She of the Throne. Teacher. Keeper of the Secret Name."

Nadia leaned back, satisfied. "Ahh. And why are you here?"

"I am here to heal. And to teach."

"Why are you here?"

Angela's eyes opened as knowledge filled her, and as she gazed at Nadia, it seemed as if everything emanated rays of light and color. "I am here to rescue my people."

Michael grunted. He came over to crouch next to Angela. "Now I understand."

"Understand what?" Nadia asked.

"Why that girl came to Angela. Her family died, but she survived. She is like Angela. Gifted. Her soul called out to her kin."

"I think that there is more to it. They share a very long history together." Nadia turned her attention back to Angela. "What is the Soul Thief?"

Angela closed her eyes again as more visions of her other life came to her. "He was my lover. He was once like us, human, only stronger." She paused. "I am his destroyer." Angela's eyes flew open as she broke trance, and she looked in shock at her great-aunt, her heart beating so strongly that it shook her body. Nadia lifted a hand to her own mouth then lowered it as she stared back at her grandniece.

"I can't do this. I can't," Angela said.

Michael put his hand on Angela's shoulder. She flinched at the sensation of human contact and then relaxed, looking up at him gratefully. Then she returned her attention to her great-aunt. "When is Granddad coming back?"

Nadia replied tranquilly, "When he has rescued Cassandra."

Angela leaped up and staggered. "What? Why didn't you tell me?"

"Because you would have rushed to help, and that thing would have captured and destroyed you. Sit down, girl."

Angela shook her head and headed for the door. Michael moved to bar her way.

"He'll eat Granddad! I have to stop him!"

Michael spread his arms as she attempted to elude him. "You're in no shape to go anywhere."

"Angela, you know he has his ways. He can come and go unseen. And I gave him something to get him past the sentinels. Sit down before you hurt yourself." Nadia waved at the couch.

Angela pushed weakly at her great-uncle, then all at once numbness washed over her limbs, and the world seemed to tilt as she collapsed. Michael helped her back to the couch, and she sat, breathing heavily as sweat dripped down her face.

"He has been gone for four hours," Nadia said. "He should be back at any time. We have watchers on every street in and out of there."

Angela hunched her shoulders, unable to move and hating herself for her weakness. At that moment, she wanted nothing more than to see her grandfather, her teacher and closest family, sitting safely beside her.

"Angel," Nadia continued. "You know he is stronger than anyone else here. When he returns we can decide what to do about that thing."

"It's all my fault. I shouldn't have told him about Cassandra. She's my... patient. My responsibility."

Nadia raised her hand, palm out. "Right now, you are your own sole responsibility. Get some rest, Angela. Lie down. We'll wake you when he gets back."

Giving in to immense exhaustion, Angela awkwardly lowered herself onto the couch, and her eyes, already heavy, closed as her awareness fled.

A timeless interval later, Angela experienced the odd sensation that the room was brilliantly lit, or perhaps that light filled her head. She could not awaken, but she could not truly sleep. She felt detached and expectant, as if she would entertain a visitor soon. The feeling grew, fueled by images of her recent trauma at the hands of the Soul Thief and by the unexpected revelations from her previous life. Then a gate to old memories quietly opened, and Angela saw in her mind's eye, more clearly than ever, the face of the man who would become the Soul Thief. His features were angular and handsome, though there was an arrogant tilt to his face that she hoped she herself lacked. Her vision expanded as she became absorbed in the experience of reliving that unimaginably distant time and life, and she saw everything.

She, the Lady of Light, was standing in the council chamber, looking down at her beloved, who stood in the center of the room. Sunshine streamed in through skylights and tall, narrow windows, tinted in rainbow colors by exquisite stained glass, and moving sculptures of crystal that hung from the ceiling.

"Aye," she found herself saying. A vote had been taken, and hers was the last to be heard. A swell of sound from all those assembled grew into a chorus of approval, and she knew that her partner had been invested in the office of Chancellor. The Lady's heart was full of pride at his accomplishment, and she smiled down at him. He turned, seeking her face, and smiled warmly back. She knew that later they would celebrate with feasting and lovemaking. By her side was the tall woman, her other partner, whom she hoped would be there as well.

The scene dissolved, and she was walking with him on a wide promenade under the stars. Fountains lit from below cast delicate light on the path and on the trees shading it to either side while the smooth stone beneath their feet shimmered with opalescence.

"Beloved. The council rejected my plan. Again." His tone was calm, but she could sense the anger within him. She placed a hand on his shoulder, but he shrugged it off.

"Surely your allies in the council see things the way you do." A cool breeze, laden with moisture, teased a hair from beneath her tall, elaborate headpiece, and she absentmindedly tucked it behind one ear.

He was silent for a moment. Then he stopped walking and turned to look at her, his hands at his belt. The Lady of Light turned to face him.

"It seems that my allies are too easily swayed by hidebound bureaucrats." He gestured eloquently with a graceful hand. "They agree that my ideas are sound, but they say I am too impatient. Give it a few years, they tell me, and the council will begin to explore my ideas." He slashed a hand downward. "They are weak! Our people have become degenerate. The council members know that our birth rate is falling, and I've told them it's because we are no longer challenged by a too-gentle world. Sooner than they think, we will fall extinct beneath the red sun, like our predecessors did so long ago. It is time we moved outward and explored the many worlds of this cosmos."

"Should we show them the newest world that I discovered? The one that lies beyond the realm of dream and death?"

"No, not yet. I hope to save that for my final presentation in three turnings. To go there is to go into exile, and they are not ready for that. But it seems I must show them something. I must find a more compelling reason for them to follow my plan." He frowned, though she was relieved to see that he no longer seemed so angry. She knew that he was a man of action, and having a plan helped to soothe his impatient heart.

"If anyone can find such a reason, you can. I will help."

He smiled at her. "Truly you are my heart's own treasure. I can always depend on you." They linked arms and continued walking.

The scene shifted again. She was in a large bedroom, and the air rang with his shouts.

"The fools! No one will see unless I force them to see!" He swept an arm across a table, scattering papers and books across the floor. He pointed a finger at the table, and a light shimmered into being.

She gasped. "No! We spoke about this. It isn't simply dangerous; this breaks the oldest laws of our people."

He glared at her as the light on the table grew brighter. "And why would you tell me what I already know, beloved?"

There was an ironic twist on the appellation, and she was afraid of him as never before. "I cannot let you take this step. If necessary, I will go to the council with what I know."

His eyes widened as he stared at her. "So you betray me,

too?" His eyes lost their focus for a moment, and she heard the door crash open behind her. She whirled, but not quickly enough. Strong hands grasped her from behind, and though several of her kicks found their mark and elicited grunts of pain, she was soon subdued. It was his private guard, who had been waiting for his unspoken signal.

She was rushed unceremoniously downstairs into one of the cells in the basement of the great house she shared with him, and she knew she would be held there while he enacted his most dangerous plan yet, one that, years ago, he had spoken of in an unguarded moment and later promised that he would never carry out.

The scene dissolved again, and then the Lady of Light and the woman she loved were shackled and gagged in the gallery above a vast dining hall. She knew he had brought them to witness the culmination of his work. She had long ago ceased struggling against her bonds.

Below, she saw a procession of notables enter the chamber where her partner, the Chancellor, and his retinue were already seated. Servants were stationed all around the perimeter of the hall with tables and trays laden with exotic viands. The dignitaries took seats at the longest table, whose head was occupied by the Chancellor and his closest advisers. Then, as the Lady of Light was scanning the length of the table, a movement caught her eye. Looking over, she saw a dark-clothed figure in the shadows on the opposite side of the room. It raised something and pointed it down at her partner. She screamed behind the muffling gag, but there was nothing she could do. There was a flash and a cracking sound, and the body of her beloved jerked in his chair and slumped. The figure turned toward her and raised his weapon. Bound as she was, the Lady of Light waited helplessly for the next shot to take her own life. There was another crack, but the expected oblivion did not descend. She saw the shadowy figure fall, and she looked down at the hall below. One of the dignitaries was lowering a similar weapon, and she realized that the assassin had been seen and dispatched. Her partner had not counted on her survival.

The scene dissolved again. She was once more in the council chamber, and she saw that several of the windows were boarded up. Others gave view onto a devastated landscape where there had once been beauty. She was standing before her own tall chair, addressing the others in the room.

"Madness, gentlemen, begins and ends in the realms that I have mapped," she said to the assembled councilors. "I have found evidence that, though fallen, the old Chancellor, my partner, has somehow secured a place for himself in the Otherworld and has launched attacks against our people's minds from there."

Several councilors began shouting simultaneously, and the new Chancellor, her woman partner who had taken office after the assassination, rapped her stone gavel sharply. "One at a time. Let the council hear from the Eastern Hold."

A stocky woman stood and placed her hands on the railing. "What is the nature of this evidence? We have only your word that such a place exists."

There was silence as everyone looked at the Lady of Light expectantly. She took a deep breath and raised her right hand in an arcane gesture. "Behold the Otherworld."

Light, sourceless and without warmth, illuminated the hall.

The shapes of stone, carven wood, tall chairs, and boarded windows faded, to be replaced with a sylvan scene of forest meadow under a brilliant noonday sun. All present found themselves standing on wild grass in a place that was dream-like and overly vivid. Most were struck silent with awe, though one or two doubled over and retched, gasping. She lowered her hand, and the scene faded, to be replaced with the prosaic hall.

The silence was profound, and all eyes were on the Lady of Light as she drew herself to her full height. "As to the evidence, I have gone to that place and I have seen his shadow, a great blanket of darkness that hid the sun. I have found the places where the minds of our people touch that world, and he has infected them with his foulness and stripped them of their reason. He has even stolen the precious talents that our people have cultivated over lifetimes, taking them for himself and perverting them." She stopped, a knotted fist in her heart stealing her voice as she contemplated the man whom she once loved who had become the bitterest enemy of her people.

A tall, thin man stood, his face drawn with weariness. The Lady said, "Speak, visitor from the River Towns."

The weary man spoke. "Why does he do this? Why betray us all into darkness and the end of our race?"

"I believe that he tests us. Before he was killed, or should I say before he gave up his body, he told me that our people had become weak and needed a challenge. In his way of thinking only the strong survive, and it is possible that he will seek to wield power over a world populated by a small remnant."

"Lady of Light, what then can we do against such weapons as he wields?"

She stiffened with resolve. "I shall bring our most talented hunters to the Otherworld. I have learned how to do this, how to carry our people bodily into that place."

There was muttering, swiftly quelled by a glare from the Chancellor. "Please continue, Lady," she said firmly.

"I have a link to him still, and with it I have learned where he conceals his greatest vulnerability," she said coldly. "We shall bring him to justice in that world before it's too late for our people and our own world."

Another councilor stood. "It is already too late. There is no justice now for our wasted world and our decimated people."

"While our world may indeed be ruined, I disagree that it is too late for us." She leaned forward, placing her hands on the railing in front of her seat. "I have found a new home for our people, a fair place untouched by this war." The council chamber was silent. "I will open a way for all of us yet alive to escape to that place. Once our enemy is finally dealt with, there will be no danger of another such devastating conflict. His talent is unique to him." She sat, and the chamber erupted with questions.

The scene shifted again. She was standing at the hill of her prior visions of the wasteland, and there was a long line of people walking slowly up to its summit. At that summit there was a shimmering of the air suggestive of a heat mirage. As people reached it, their bodies dissolved. The wasteland stank with the odor of burning, and many of the faces she saw were set in grim desperation, but their discipline overcame their fear as each, in turn, entered the portal.

She turned to her lover, the Chancellor, who stood by her

side, fingers entwined with her own.

"This is the last of us," the Lady of Light said.

"What is your plan now?"

She sighed. "Our enemy is imprisoned and his name taken from him, but without a jailer he will soon break free of his bonds. I have bound myself with an oath to ensure that he does not do so. I will exile myself to the Otherworld to ensure the safety of our people."

The Chancellor stared into her face, eyes glittering with unshed tears. "You have lost so much. Your name will live forever in our hearts for what you have done and will do. And my heart will never mend."

The Lady of Light shook her head. "Nothing lasts forever. One day I too will be reborn into the new world, and on that day he will be released to seek his freedom. In that life I shall execute his final judgment, whether it is for life everlasting or for death and a final ending. And I shall find you then, wherever you are." She reached to touch her lover's face and gazed deeply into her eyes, storing the memory of it in her most secret self.

To her mind came a vision of that new world, with its blue skies, green, verdant plains, and rushing rivers, and from within the dream memory, Angela recognized that it was earth. Her people had transmigrated into the physical forms of the dominant hominid species of that time and had become the progenitors of all humanity.

The memory faded, along with her sense of being embodied, and as she drifted in the space of hypnagogic sleep, Angela felt anguish at the vast gulf of time separating her from her people. The memory of herself standing in the desolate wasteland was, she knew, the last moment she experienced as a physical being before entering the Otherworld to guard the Soul Thief.

When Angela was born into the new world, he was freed. When he had attacked Cassandra's mother he had been seeking Angela, and the convergence of their paths seemed, in retrospect, to be foreordained. Clothing himself with the soul stuff of humans, he had the power to step fully into physical form. But why hadn't he simply declared victory? What did he still need from Angela?

A timeless time passed as the strange, inward light dissipated, and Angela tried to awaken. Something prevented her, though. A brief vision of the wasteland appeared and vanished before she could see what occupied its center. Another, longer image appeared, and another, and she realized she was seeing the Soul Thief, and she felt a chill of fear. He held something in his right hand. Coming closer with each flash, Angela finally saw that it was George's head he held by the hair, its face twisted in a grimace of horror.

Angela sat bolt upright, a shout echoing in her ears. She was in a dark bedroom, and had evidently been brought there while she was unconscious. She heard voices in the living room, but none were raised in concern, so her shout must have been entirely in her mind. She got out of bed and crept to the partially open door to listen, feeling an unaccountable need for her wakefulness to be unnoticed.

"Something is wrong." It was Michael. "George has been gone six hours. One of the boys thought he saw him walking away from the hospital, but there was nothing when he went to check."

"I'd know if my brother was in trouble," Nadia replied. "Now I'm sure of it."

There was a pause, then Michael spoke forcefully. "Keep looking." He must have been on the phone. "No! Don't try to get closer to the hospital... *Marel tu o Del!*"

Angela heard the phone being slammed down, its bells ringing slightly. Michael was grumbling.

"Michael, they will do what they will do," said Nadia.

"They are fools to approach that creature."

Angela sat back on the bed. She had no choice. George was in trouble, and she was the only one who had a chance of finding him, though the thought of getting closer to the Soul Thief made her want to crawl into a box and hide for the rest of her life. However, her fear for her grandfather shoved that thought out of her mind. First, though, she had to discover whether she had any of her paranormal skills left. Knowing that her great-uncle and great-aunt would try to prevent her from leaving, she decided to try George's invisibility trick. Even if she were successful, she was afraid her great-aunt would see through it, so she needed to find a way to distract Nadia.

First she arranged her pillows and bedclothes to resemble her own sleeping form. Then she closed her eyes and imagined herself surrounded by a thick black cloud. She chanted the key words in her mind, and the ensuing rush of power was gratify-ingly potent. Perhaps it was her fear that powered her spell, or it could be that the Soul Thief had inadvertently opened up new reservoirs of strength.

The conversation from outside the room was muted, as if Angela's ears were stuffed with cotton. She opened her eyes; the light streaming around the door was watery and thin. What she could see of the room seemed two-dimensional, flat, and washed out. She rose from the bed quietly, pushed the door open, and crept down the hallway to pause at the threshold to the living room. Michael was standing by the phone, frowning, and Nadia was in her chair. Neither looked in her direction.

She turned and quietly made her way to the opposite end of the trailer where Nadia's bedroom was located. The door was partly ajar, and she went in, but warily. Her great-aunt had an uncanny ability to sense everything that happened in her home, and Angela was afraid of alerting her. But Michael and Nadia kept talking in those muffled tones.

Angela went to the large window that faced the front yard, carefully unlatched it, and slid it open, feeling an upsurge of anxiety as she touched the sash. As Angela had suspected, Nadia had erected a psychic barrier to prevent her escape. Leaving the window open, Angela tiptoed quietly back to her room and waited. Soon, a cool breeze wafted down the hallway, as she had hoped it would. She heard a gasp from the living room.

"Nadia? What's wrong?" Michael asked.

There was a pause. "Go check on Angela, will you?"

Angela heard his footsteps, and her door opened wider to allow light to stream in. Michael peered at her bed, a puzzled frown on his face. Then he glanced farther down the hall and cursed, ducking out of the room, and she let out a breath she had not realized she was holding. She heard his footsteps rapidly receding, and then she saw him run back toward the living room.

"Nadia! She has escaped through your bedroom window."

"Impossible! I have a ward on the windows that would freeze her cold with fear. Georgie taught her the invisibility trick, and I'm not about to let her sneak out of here and get herself killed."

"I will look anyway."

Angela heard the front door slam open as Nadia squawked in protest. She crept along the hallway and paused before entering the living room. The door was still partly ajar, and Angela gathered her courage. She darted to the door and pulled it open. Nadia looked directly at her and shouted, trying to stand up, but Angela slipped outside. As she passed through the doorway, however, she felt a cold shiver down her spine and everything snapped back into focus. Nadia's urgent shouts to Michael grew abruptly louder.

Angela ran out to the road and dashed over to Michael's car. The driver's side was unlocked, so she jerked the door open and threw herself into the seat.

"No, Angela!" Michael's pounding footsteps grew near as Angela reached under the dash to grope for the dangling wires that she knew were there. The engine started with a roar, and Angela stomped on the accelerator. She caught a glimpse of Michael in the rearview mirror, chasing her and then throwing his hands in the air.

"Sorry, Nana, Michael," Angela muttered. "Granddad, I'm coming to get you."

Angela neared the hospital. There was a lot of traffic in the city that night, and Angela drove carefully. Consequently, when a group of pedestrians stepped in front of her, she slammed on the brakes to avoid running them down. However, they did not move out of the way and ignored her honking horn.

"Dammit!"

She smacked the steering wheel in frustration. She noticed that the pedestrians' faces were slack, and they stared blankly ahead as they walked slowly across the intersection toward the hospital. Other car horns chorused with hers, and one driver next to her chirped his wheels to express his urgency, but the somnambulant people didn't react. Angela took a deep breath, held it, and released it, forcibly relaxing her muscles. They were under a psychic influence; she was convinced of that.

Then, without warning, the crushing onslaught of mind control made her cry out in agony. She pushed back hard, and the contest raged for several minutes before the attack ended, leaving her gasping. It was undoubtedly the Soul Thief, and she wondered if he was truly aware of her or if he was simply broadcasting powerful telepathic commands to everyone in the area. Hoping that the latter was true, she gripped the wheel and, closing her eyes, wove the sense-befuddling invisibility charm. Sound receded from her awareness, and when she opened her eyes, she saw the familiar darkening effect in her visual field, more pronounced than ever before.

The pedestrians finished crossing, and she pulled forward, acutely aware that, under the charm, she was much more likely to be hit by other drivers if she didn't watch carefully. Angela began running an obstacle course, dodging oblivious pedestrians and vehicles as she neared the hospital. No one attempted to blockade her, though, and she arrived unnoticed.

Unworried about finding a parking space, she double-parked the old Buick in the circular driveway in front of the emergency entrance, where she saw a long line of people on the sidewalk, waiting to enter. She got out of the car cautiously and, approaching the line, noticed that they were silent, shuffling their feet as one by one they entered the hospital. Their faces were slack, their eyes staring blankly. Angela was certain that the same force that had attempted to dominate her was drawing them in. She crept alongside the queue then cut through the line toward another unused entry door. Peering through the inset glass window, she observed that the lights were not on in the foyer. She opened the door and slipped in.

Though the foyer was dark, the emergency power provided a glowering red illumination. The line of people proceeded past the emergency admissions desk and through the inner security door, which gave access to the medical facilities. Wishing to avoid any further contact with the entranced people, Angela went to the door that led to the administrative wing and entered, senses keen for any alarm.

The corridor was dark, and an acrid stench of smoke made her eyes water. Sidling along the wall, alert for danger, she found a door that connected with the secure ward. She tested it, found it to be unlocked, and carefully pushed it open. Before she could enter, an ear-piercing shriek caused her to slam herself against the wall, breathing heavily. She peered around the open entry into the hallway and barely suppressed a gasp. A nurse lay on a gurney, pinned to it by hundreds of hypodermic needles driven through the flesh of her arms and legs. Other moans and cries reverberated through the hallways. Then a shadow passed through, and the scene melted and deformed, revealing a Hieronymus Bosch–like snapshot of an enormous, hellish orgy before the hospital corridor became visible again. The Soul Thief had used his stolen gift to bring his own version of the Otherworld to the earthly realm.

Angela crept to the side of the nurse and reached over to try pulling needles out of her arm. When she grasped the first one, the woman's head lifted, and her eyes focused on Angela, though she should have been invisible. "Please don't. I need that medication."

Angela stopped, her hand shaking. The nurse smiled and lay back. There came another one of the piercing screams. Angela saw that it came from a patient farther down the hall who was sitting on the floor, pinching himself and shrieking. She realized that there was no help she could offer those people as long as the Soul Thief reigned. The only thing she could do was stick to her mission and hope that, with her grandfather's help, she could defeat the enemy. Having made that decision, Angela closed her eyes and sought her link with her grandfather. Her mind filled with an image of George, strapped into a medical exam chair that had been tilted back.

Angela opened her eyes and continued moving down the corridor. A faint sound, like a dull roaring, became audible. She turned a corner and saw another patient strapped into a bed. Ginny was standing over the patient with a blowtorch and was waving it over her arm. The patient screamed in anguish as her flesh blackened and smoked. Angela rushed forward to stop the torture, but a rippling veil of colors passed over the scene, causing it to vanish along with most of the corridor. Suddenly she was teetering on the precipice above a vast, smoke-filled abyss, but she caught herself and stumbled back.

The abyssal scene disappeared to reveal the hallway, but with no sign of Ginny or the patient. Angela closed her eyes and concentrated and was rewarded with a clearer vision of George. He was inert. She opened her eyes and began moving again.

A tapping sound echoed down the darkened hallway. Angela searched all around for the source until she saw, behind her, a hunched person with a walking stick shuffling toward her. Angela pulled back as the stranger approached, and as the person came even with her, she saw that it was the old woman from the Otherworld. The woman paused and peered, squinting, at Angela.

"Lost your little friend, lady?" She cackled. "Time is your friend. The old one dies and the new one is born." Her eyes were bright with amusement.

"I found my past. Now I need to find my grandfather. But aren't you Nana?"

The woman waved her stick irritably. "He's not important now. Nor am I. Look for your friend. She needs your love."

The woman vanished in a cloud of steam that filled the hall. When the cloud cleared, the door to an empty treatment room was open in front of Angela. She heard a voice behind her that she knew very well.

"Thank you, nurse. I'll take it from here," said Eric.

Angela whirled around, but two burly orderlies, one of

whom she recognized as the Buddhist James McTavish, pinned her arms to her side. She struggled and tried to scream, but one of the orderlies forced a huge cotton gag into her mouth. Eric was standing in front of her with a hypo and a friendly smile.

"This will sting a little. Then you'll fall asleep." He plunged the needle into her arm and everything went away.

12.

FIRST SHE became aware of moaning and yelps of pain. Then her vision returned, though at first she wasn't sure if she was still partially blind, as her surroundings were shadowy and indistinct. She realized it was a treatment room, but it had grown vast, far larger than any room in the hospital she knew. Dark figures moved among several of the beds.

Angela attempted to shift and realized that she was strapped into a bed. Thrashing futilely against the bindings, she lifted her head and saw a tube from a bandage on her left arm that led to an IV stand. She fought the lingering effects of the sedative. One of the figures approached, and as it neared, she recognized Eric. After glancing incuriously at her, he checked the IV drip.

"Eric...?" She coughed. "Eric! It's me, Angela. What're you doing?"

Eric grasped her wrist to check her pulse and spoke without looking at her face. "That's nice. I have a friend named Angela."

Angela struggled again. "Eric! I am Angela, your friend. Let me out of this bed this instant."

He put a hand to her eyelid to check her dilation. She turned her head against his grip and glared at him. "Remember at the dance club? I told you I was losing faith in my work. It's me."

Eric stopped moving, and his eyes widened. "You sound like her. But you look nothing like my friend. I'm sorry, but I have to sedate you now or you may hurt yourself."

He went to the tray to prep a sedative for the drip. Something was wrong with him. He wasn't acting like the Eric she knew. Then she realized that, though she had lost consciousness, some portion of her invisibility spell was somehow still in effect and was interfering with his perception of her. She stilled herself, closed her eyes, and concentrated, and the shadowy nature of the room receded as the light grew stronger.

"Look at me, Eric."

He glanced at her and did an almost comical double take. "Angela!" He set the sedative down and started fumbling with her straps.

"It is you. I'm so sorry! The boss told everyone he wants to see you if you show up. How'd you get in here? The hospital is on lockdown."

She struggled to sit as the straps were released. "There's no time to talk now. Can you see what's happening here?"

He nodded as he withdrew the IV needle from her arm. "Yes. The hospital had an emergency, but it's all under control now. Central sent a bunch of us to help. Aren't you glad?"

She shook her head. "But there are patients and nurses being tortured."

"Angela, honey." He looked at her with his familiar grin. "You should know better. The boss wouldn't let anything like that happen here. That's crazy talk." He helped her to her feet.

She grasped his arm. "I'm looking for someone. Two some-ones. There's Cassandra, remember her? She would be known as patient C. She's in one of the treatment rooms." She let go and started for the door. "And there's my grandfather, George. Big, white haired, beard. He came here to arrange her release."

"I think patient C is under the boss's care now. I haven't seen your grandfather, though."

Angela stopped and turned to him. "Then I've got to find him. Come on, help me out."

He grinned. "I'm sure the boss would know where George is. He's been doing a great job managing this hospital."

Angela looked him in the eyes and shuddered when she saw a blank indifference that had never been there in all the years that she had known him. Her best friend was possessed by the Soul Thief.

Pushing aside the grief that threatened to overwhelm her with that realization, she gauged the distance to the door. When Eric's head was turned, she dashed for the door and flung it open. James and the other orderly stood on the other side of the doorway, and they grabbed her arms.

"I'm sorry," Eric said. "I had to call them. The boss said you would need to be persuaded."

She was incredulous. "I didn't see you call them."

He laughed. "But I did. Everything is so much easier now that the boss is in charge." He and the orderlies escorted Angela out of the room.

Eric knocked on Josef's office door and paused. Then he opened the door without waiting for an audible reply. Angela was manhandled into the room by the orderlies, but Eric waited outside.

"Boss, she's here," he called out.

Her eyes widened in horror as she saw the room's occupant. Cassandra was seated at the desk, dressed in Josef's clothing.

She smiled.

"Cassie? But..."

Cassandra stood and came around the desk. "You know who I am. How charming to see you again." Her voice was that of the teenager, but the cadences were horribly familiar.

"No!" Angela wailed. She struggled again, and the orderlies fought to hold her still. Cassandra stepped closer and touched her face. Angela froze, horrified.

"But no. Your beloved Cassandra is not at home." The Soul Thief laughed and pointed to one corner of the room. "Look who I found."

Angela looked to her left where it pointed. She felt as if she had been punched in the stomach. "Granddad!"

George was strapped to a mobile treatment chair. He appeared to be unconscious. Angela pulled against the grip of the orderlies and glared at the Soul Thief. "If you've hurt him..."

It smiled. "He sleeps. As is proper for someone who tried to take something from me." Its borrowed face contorted. "From me! I lost everything because of you! No one may take from me again." It calmed again. "But come. Sit. We must discuss something dear to me."

The orderlies led Angela to another chair, and they bound her with portable restraints. The Soul Thief sat back down and rolled the office chair closer. "You. You are dear to me."

"What are you talking about?"

"You have something of mine. It's a small thing, but without it I am still not free." It touched her on the forehead, and she flinched.

"Your soul," it said, tenderly. "Your beautiful, light-filled soul. You are named Angela in this life. I found that to be fitting. An angel of mercy."

Angela snarled, "Not for you. If you could have taken my soul, you would have already."

The Soul Thief ignored her. "When you bound me into that dream-world prison, it was the power of your soul that trapped me. Most of my life is still there. I must have my freedom, and only by taking your soul will I be able to guarantee it. You must offer it freely in order for that to happen."

Angela glared at the enemy, mute with rage.

"I will free your dear grandfather in exchange. If you refuse..."

Angela sagged, the wind knocked out of her. She turned her head and looked at her grandfather, who looked so small and frail in the chair, and a tear trickled down her cheek. All of the memories of her life under his care flooded back to her, and she discovered a profound sense of peace and generosity that filled her with new strength.

"I will save you, Granddad," Angela said softly. She looked at the Soul Thief. "How do I know you won't simply kill him when I give you what you want?"

Her enemy looked into her eyes. "I don't need him or what he has. You are the only one I care about now. I swear by my power that I will release him when you have offered your soul to me."

Angela remembered that such an oath was truly binding for her people and decided that she had to trust that he would fulfill it. "Okay. You may take what you need."

It laughed with delight and waved a hand at George. "Boys,

take that away."

Angela yelped in shock.

"He's free. Fortunately for me, he's also dead."

"No!"

"And you're mine."

The Soul Thief reached over and touched Angela's forehead more firmly. The world swirled, a deep hum filled her mind, and Angela was propelled into the Otherworld.

Angela was standing in a clearing, and her head spun from the abrupt, disorienting transition. It took a moment for her to realize that it was her own meadow. There was the small lean-to where she kept her walking staff, but the rest of the space had changed dramatically. The last time she had been there, the grass had been short and the trees friendly and verdant with new growth. Now, shadows crowded the eaves of moss-laden trees surrounding a meadow overgrown with weeds, and tangled undergrowth vied with huge, multicolored fungi, making it nearly impossible for her to see any path into the forest.

She felt her focus dragged inexorably upward, and she saw the vast, spinning vortex of darkness that heralded the Soul Thief. In that moment, she was crushed to her knees by the immense pressure exerted by her enemy, and she could feel her sense of self shrinking. Mustering her dwindling strength, Angela gritted her teeth and pushed back against that pressure. For what seemed like an aeon, she and the Soul Thief were locked in a stalemate, while the vortex growled impotently above. Then, with breathtaking suddenness, the pressure lifted, and Angela nearly collapsed with relief.

Bright daylight flooded into the meadow. Lifting her head, Angela saw the Soul Thief in the body of Cassandra at the other side of the clearing. Its voice came clearly to her.

"It appears that you are able to resist me even now." It paused, as if considering its words carefully. Then, in a deeper voice it said, "By the power by which we are all bound, I hold you to your promise."

The Soul Thief raised something in one hand. It was her walking staff. Angela felt an overwhelming hunger to possess the staff once again, and she found herself walking toward the Soul Thief. Realizing that some enchantment was controlling her actions, she attempted to stop but could not. It was as if she could not think of anything better to do. She struggled to pierce the fog of bland acceptance that pushed her toward her doom. "You lied to me."

"I did not," it replied lightly. "I released him from the world. He has gone to his destiny."

As she felt her feet shuffle toward her enemy, a memory arose of the times when the two of them had danced together, harmoniously and effortlessly. The enjoyment of that dancing had accompanied her to Earth, she knew now. Her fight to exert her will, coupled with that memory, transformed her movements, and she began dancing, slowly and gracefully, rather than walking straight toward the creature. To her surprise, she found that it was easier to resist the compulsion that had fallen on her. The Soul Thief lifted an eyebrow and smiled in appreciation.

"You are so beautiful. You always loved to dance. Soon we will be joined. I will take your light. I promise you, it will not hurt. Sweet oblivion is your reward."

Angela suppressed an urge to run in panic, knowing that it would cause her to run straight toward that promised oblivion. Executing a pirouette instead, she asked, "Why are you torturing all those people?"

The Soul Thief chuckled. "Food, my love. A body must eat to survive. But don't worry. When I am free, I won't need them anymore."

An image flashed briefly in Angela's mind. It was the Soul Thief in the Otherworld, in his own form, kneeling in chains before a tribunal seated in tall chairs. They were on a grass-covered knoll overlooking the sea, and she recognized the place from her dream-walk in childhood when she had encountered the animal boy. The Soul Thief tilted his head to look at her as she sat in one of the chairs, and though his face was haggard and his frame bony and wasted, his eyes still burned with a vast energy that pinned her to her seat. The vision dissolved.

Angela heard herself speaking. "You were condemned to remain in this place."

Its face twisted. "Forever! That is no just sentence."

As Angela danced nearer her enemy, the Soul Thief began to mimic her movement, as if her own dance compelled it to do so. She wondered briefly why it didn't just walk over to steal her soul. Perhaps there were constraints on its powers because of her resistance to it earlier. With that hopeful thought, she refocused on fighting for her life.

The two of them were now circling in an elaborate approach while darkness obscured the clearing.

"But why Cassandra? Who was she to you?" Angela tried to

keep the Soul Thief talking, postponing the inevitable.

Its voice was bleak. "You loved her more than you loved me. I am not accustomed to sharing. I take what is due me."

Angela stooped in an elaborate sweeping move that brought her hand close to the ground to try to grasp something—anything—that she could use as a weapon, but her scrabbling fingers found nothing in the wild grass. She danced, sweating with the effort of resistance. "Why do you still call me 'beloved'?"

The Soul Thief's eyes registered surprise, and its step faltered. "Because I still love you. And now that you are flesh again, I shall take your soul into my own and live once more."

Angela saw another memory of the two of them, so vivid that it overlaid the meadow. They were walking hand in hand in a beautiful valley.

"We had love," her enemy said in a huge voice that came from everywhere.

"But you destroyed it. Why did you destroy us all?" she cried.

The Soul Thief of her vision stopped walking and turned to her. "For you, beloved. I wanted to give everything to you. A strong world with you by my side, immortal and invulnerable."

The vision dissolved, and Angela felt a pang of anguish. She found that she could stop moving toward the Soul Thief as the force that compelled her relented for a moment. She looked intently at her enemy, seeing in the physical face of Cassandra a hint of the love of that man in her memory. Its eyes widened, and it ducked its head, flinching away from something in her gaze. Then the Soul Thief snarled and raised the staff once again, renewing the compulsion. Angela resumed her dance.

As she moved closer to her glowering enemy, she felt the personality of her past self growing within her, shedding the ephemera of her earthly life and filling her with knowledge. It was as if she were awakening from a deep sleep, as doors opened onto memories of the years of study from which she had gleaned the hidden knowledge of the Otherworld. She knew that, in the Otherworld, all memories still lived, and all times, past, present and future, were joined in timelessness.

Along with that knowledge came the realization that those whom her enemy had supplanted still existed in the Otherworld, and she gasped. Dizzy with hope, yet afraid to admit it, Angela closed her eyes and thought of those whom she had lost.

Granddad? Are you here?

There was no answer that she could discern, and her dance faltered. Then, as her past self continued to assert its presence, her feelings for the woman of her dreams and of that lifetime, who had become Chancellor, arose within her. That woman had been reborn as Cassandra, she knew now, and their reunion had served to awaken Angela to her true self. Cassandra must be the "friend" that the old woman had told her to seek. Yearning for her once and future beloved, with her dance Angela expressed herself in the wordless language of desire.

"Cassandra?" she whispered. She could finally admit to the love that she felt, a love deepened by her own far memories, and she allowed it to fill her unconditionally. She opened her eyes to see, with a pang, the physical form of Cassandra scowling with anger.

The Soul Thief clenched its fists, all sardonic amusement gone. "Talk to me! The child is gone."

And then a voice came upon the wind. "Angela."

Light and warmth grew in Angela's chest, penetrating the shadows under the branches of the forest, until by its illumination she saw the shimmering form of Cassandra under those trees. Standing by her side was the ghostly form of George, a protective hand on Cassandra's shoulder. Tears blocked Angela's view, and the final puzzle piece fitted smoothly into place. In the Otherworld, love was the highest law, and it bound all souls, both of the living and of the dead.

The pain and hatred aroused by the Soul Thief dissolved within her, and Angela realized that she had always had the power to release the last chains that bound him here. Such freedom would allow him to move on to the destination of all souls on the wheel of forgetfulness and rebirth.

Angela and the spirit of Cassandra, by unspoken agreement, converged on the enemy. It started to back away but became tangled in the tall grass. "What are you doing? You are bound by your promise!" the Soul Thief said, waving its hands, Cassandra's hands, in woven gestures of arcane potency. But no power wielded by the Soul Thief could touch Angela anymore.

"And I will keep that promise. Beloved, I forgive you."

The Soul Thief whimpered as it tried to escape. The light in the clearing was growing steadily, and a wind whipped the trees.

"Cassie," Angela said calmly. "Come to me. Join me."

She and the ghostly form of Cassandra caught up with the stumbling, retreating Soul Thief. The Soul Thief screamed, and the scream blended with a shout of ecstasy from Angela and from Cassandra. The three of them merged in an embrace as Angela kissed Cassandra, and the radiance emanating from the kiss illuminated the clearing with blinding brilliance.

WAKE

WHEN I open my eyes
And I see you
And I hear your voice
My whole body smiles
- C

EPILOGUE

THE UBIQUITOUS San Francisco fog swirled in eddies around the tombstones, reminding Angela of the surreal Otherworld in the way that it softened the shapes of distant trees and created a stark contrast with the nearby hard-edged stone.

"Dust to dust..." She barely registered the words, heard too many times in the three days since her return to the hospital. Yet those words were said over the mortal remains of her grandfather, and she felt a knot clench her throat briefly.

Nadia was the first one to step forward with a handful of soil, which she tossed down into the open grave. Next was Michael, followed by her cousins on that side of the family. Angela was the last in line.

"You know, we were becoming friends," said Eric. Dressed in what was for him the unthinkable—a formal black suit—and topped with a shock of platinum hair, he had the look of a forlorn rock star. He jammed his hands into his pockets and sighed.

Angela reached behind and hugged him with one arm. "I knew someday you would be. He was kind of old-fashioned, but he was also wise and generous."

She suppressed a completely out-of-place chuckle. Yesterday, she had gone on a dream-walk and had met George's oversoul. There, she had learned of what had transpired between him and Eric, and they had shared a laugh over what he acknowledged had been a narrow point of view.

He had also told her to go talk to Nadia when Angela questioned him about his nature. When Angela had asked her great-aunt about oversouls, she had learned that everyone had a deeper self that, at death, would absorb one's personality into itself again. Nadia had been fascinated to learn that Angela could communicate directly with those entities. However, upon learning that Angela had visited her grandfather's oversoul, she strongly cautioned that such interactions could bind his spirit to the world of the living, and he would become a mulo, a restless ghost. Angela decided to keep her future visits to George a secret.

It was her turn. Stepping forward with her clot of dirt, Angela looked down on the casket, paused for a moment, then tossed. Dusting her hands on her black skirt, she offered thanks to the part of him that she knew was watching.

The chorus of sobs offered a mournful accompaniment to the work of burial as Angela stepped back to join the crowd of family and friends. She found herself wrapped in one warm hug after another as they departed the gravesite and walked together to the waiting hearses and brightly painted cars and caravans of her Rom family.

"Dear child, are you going to be okay?" Nadia had come to walk beside Angela. She looked at her grandniece with concern as she put a hand on her shoulder.

Angela turned to her and looked into those eyes, so much like her grandfather's. "Nana, I'll be fine. I want to get back to the hospital. So many lives were shattered by what happened." She paused, wondering how much more she could say.

Nadia smiled. "And there's Cassandra."

"Yes," Angela acknowledged. She knew that Nadia understood. She felt relieved that she would not need to explain her profound connection with her former patient or the intimate relationship that expressed that connection. Angela hugged Nadia and then made her way back to her car.

"Can I get a lift?" Eric hurried over.

"Sure. Drop you off at Central?"

"No, take me to Franklin." They got in. Angela raised an eyebrow, and Eric continued. "You need some help, and I volunteered to stay."

Angela shook her head, amazed. "After all you went through." Her eyes were wet with tears. She dabbed at her face and started the car.

Eric laughed. "Hell, it's the least I can do."

Six months later

Angela was seated at her desk. Staring out the window, Ginny waited as she signed a form. "There. Josef's release." Angela handed it to her friend.

"He'll be happy to go home. Oh, and Eric called to say 'hi.' He didn't want to disturb you, but he asked me to pass on his congratulations." Ginny turned to leave, but she stopped at the door and looked back.

"Angela. About Cassandra..."

"She's doing much better now. Dr. Williams says she made a real breakthrough last week. He told me he expects to sign her release in another month or so." Angela picked absentmindedly at her teeth. "I've already moved her things to the boat."

"It's going to be cozy." Ginny's lips quirked in a half smile.

Angela shrugged. "If we can survive this, we can get through anything. Besides, we've got the world's biggest front porch in case one of us feels cramped."

"No kidding. So. Tonight at eight at Nadia's?"

"Yep. Better bring your dancing shoes this time." Angela laughed. Ginny laughed, too. Angela continued, "I'm going to the meeting in a few minutes. Can you be there, too?"

"Of course." Ginny nodded and left. Angela took up another sheaf of papers and started sorting through it.

Several staffers were seated at the table in the meeting room. They looked up as Angela entered. Ginny was already there, and she raised her hand in a little wave.

"I'm sorry to keep you waiting," Angela said. "This won't take long." Taking a seat near the head of the table, she turned to one of the doctors, a distinguished-looking older man with glasses. "Robert, do you have the paperwork?"

"Yes, Dr. Cooper, right here."

He pushed across a sheaf of papers. Angela bent, flipped rapidly through them, and signed several forms.

"There. Robert, congratulations. You're the new head of psychiatry."

The others at the table applauded politely. One of them, a dark-suited woman, beamed at Angela. "Dr. Cooper, the board can't thank you enough for all the work you've done." She raised her hand as Angela opened her mouth. "No, you deserve the lion's share of the credit. You virtually single-handedly put everything back together after the terrible accident here. You could have this job in a heartbeat. Do you mind my asking why you turned it down?"

Angela paused, half smiling, then inclined her head. "Carla, I was once told that I can't abandon my past. Well, I have a complex heritage that ties me to a very special community. I've decided to honor that community by serving them. I'm starting a clinic in the East Bay, as some of you know already. Maybe there I can rediscover who I am."

"That's a high calling, Angela," Carla replied. "All the best of luck to you."

Angela shook hands all around as everyone rose to their feet in a flood of farewells, and she left the room without a backward glance. She wended her way through the busy corridor to the elevator, and as she rode it down, she began humming to herself. Tonight there would be dancing.

She exited the elevator and strode through the waiting room, and no one appeared to notice her. She might as well have been invisible. She smiled a genuine smile and left the building.

THE END